PUP SQUAD ALPHA, VOLUME 1

Vampires' Witness
Demon's Embrace

Abby Blake

MENAGE EVERLASTING

Siren Publishing, Inc.
www.SirenPublishing.com

A SIREN PUBLISHING BOOK
IMPRINT: Ménage Everlasting

PUP SQUAD ALPHA, VOLUME 1
Vampires' Witness
Demon's Embrace
Copyright © 2012 by Abby Blake

ISBN: 978-1-62241-336-2

First Printing: September 2012

Vampires' Witness
Demon's Embrace
      Cover design © Les Byerley
Print cover design by Siren-BookStrand
All art and logo copyright © 2012 by Siren Publishing, Inc.

Printed in the U.S.A.

PUBLISHER
Siren Publishing, Inc.
www.SirenPublishing.com

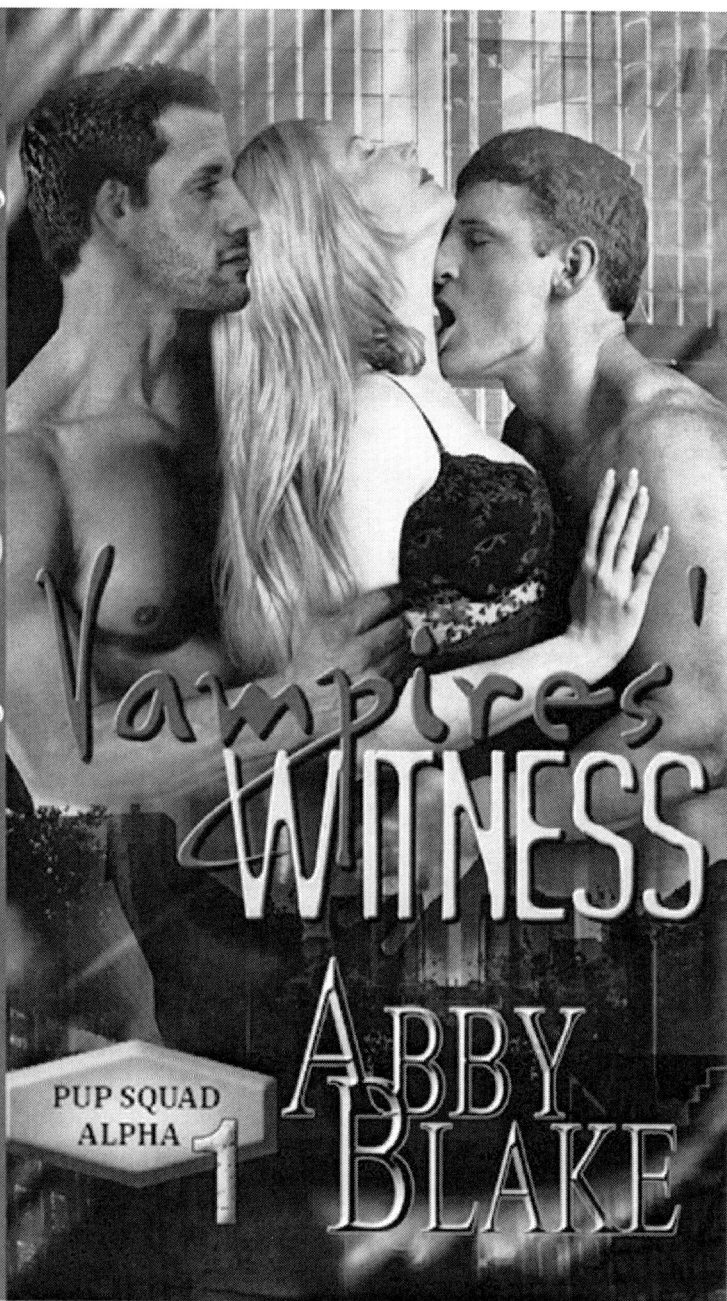

SIREN
Publishing

Ménage Everlasting

Vampires'
WITNESS

PUP SQUAD
ALPHA 1

ABBY
BLAKE

VAMPIRES' WITNESS

PUP Squad Alpha 1

ABBY BLAKE
Copyright © 2012

Chapter One

Skye Hastings took a quick glance over her shoulder, saw the foyer still empty, and turned back to the table. She couldn't explain why she'd agreed to meet her sister in this poorly lit, overly loud dance club. Jennifer knew how much she hated socializing. If her being late was some kind of plan to get Skye out and meeting people, her sister was in for one very short, heated response—hell, no!

"Hello, beautiful," a man said as he slid onto the stool beside her.

"Hi," Skye managed to force past her lips as she tried not to gag. She'd met overconfident sleazebags before, but this guy took the cake. Just the tone of his voice set her on edge. Trying very hard to not show her distaste—maybe he'd mistaken her for someone he knew—she turned to face him with a polite excuse on her lips. He was tall, very tall. Even with him sitting she had to tilt her head way back just to make eye contact. "I'm…um…waiting for someone."

"And now I'm here."

Ack! Did that line ever work for him? Feeling claustrophobic with the wall behind her and the man towering over her in front, Skye tried very hard not to show her panic. Being cornered in a nightclub was not her idea of a good time. She tilted sideways, trying to see around the man, and hopefully catch a glimpse of her sister.

The guy mirrored her movement, blocking her line of sight. "It's okay, beautiful," he said, leaning over her to run a finger down her cheek, "you and I are going to get better acquainted."

Skye shuddered at the unwelcome contact and managed to force out the word "no." She shook her head quickly, and then, giving up all pretense of being polite, slid off the stool and tried to push her way past him. It was like trying to push through a solid wall. The man laughed, obviously very aware of Skye's fear.

"Sit down. Be quiet," the man said in a mild voice. Unbelievably, Skye did exactly as she was told. Still trying to understand why she would react to the man's order the way she had, her eyes almost rolled into the back of her head when the man leaned in. At first it looked like he might try to kiss her, but all he did was lower his face to the side of her neck and breathe deeply. "Yes, beautiful, you're going to taste as good as you look."

She wanted to ask what he meant, but her mouth didn't seem to be working. She wanted to leap off the chair, scream for help, and thump the guy until he let her past.

But she did none of it.

She sat on the stool, staring at the man, her heart pounding a wild, terrified tattoo as her body seemed to somehow disobey her commands.

"About time you showed up," the tall man said to a painfully thin guy who broke through the crowd and took the stool on the other side of the table.

The new man shrugged. "Thought I saw someone I knew," he said without taking his gaze off Skye. After eyeing her for what felt like an eternity, the new man licked his lips and leaned forward to press a wet, cold kiss to her neck. Internally shuddering in revulsion, Skye still couldn't explain her physical outward calm. She hoped like hell this was a nightmare because she really, *really* wanted to wake up.

"Where's Ritchie?"

"Said he'd meet us out back. Had his eye on some redhead."

Both men laughed as if they shared a joke and then turned their attention back to her.

"I gotta say, you sure know how to pick 'em. She's real pretty."

The older man smiled. "And she's O-neg, healthy, obviously takes care of herself—she should taste mighty fine."

The younger man snorted, but nodded in agreement. "Hell, yeah. Way better than some stick-thin redhead with freckles who supposedly looks a little like his ex. When the fuck is he gonna get over his obsession with someone who's been dead for decades?"

"Don't know," the tall man said with a laugh. "You'd think seventy years would cure him of the need for revenge. But hey, if it means we don't have to share the prime catches, let the guy have his fun."

"True," the skinny man said with a laugh. "Come on, bitch. I'm hungry."

The tall man held out a hand to help her off the stool. Practically screaming inside her mind, but unable to force her body to work, Skye watched dumfounded as her arm lifted and she placed her hand in his.

"Smile," the other man said as he came up behind her. The tall man led her through the crowd toward the back of the club as she smiled serenely on the outside and screamed in terror on the inside.

The cold wrapped around her as they stepped into the alley, but even though the chill attacked her skin like a thousand little needles, she didn't even shiver. She could still feel the stupid smile plastered on her face, the unwanted expression even more agonizing by the fact that no one inside had noticed that she was leaving against her will.

She heard a couple of people approach and for one brief moment prayed for rescue. A pale man with straggly blond hair and a painfully thin red-haired woman with freckles wearing the exact same smile as Skye stepped into the tiny circle of pale light. Skye felt tears well in her eyes. Obviously this was the man they'd been talking about, and not the help she desperately needed.

"Shhh, none of that," the older man said as he wiped away the lone tear that managed to escape. "I promise you this won't hurt." But he ruined his reassurance by adding, "Of course I can't promise the same for her."

And then as they watched the third man torture the silent red-haired woman, they stood behind Skye, caressing her frozen body with their cold hands. After several minutes of sheer terror, one of them threaded a hand into her hair and pulled her head back until she was staring into the night sky. A cowardly part of her welcomed the reprieve, unable to watch the young woman being tortured a moment longer, but then both men bit into either side of her throat and reality lost all meaning.

* * * *

Benjamin Carrington followed his squad partner into the busy nightclub. Thomas was the best tracker in the business, but with so many vampires clustered in the one small area it was proving harder than expected to track them all down.

"Fuck," Thomas whispered quietly enough that only Benjamin would hear him. "I'm getting at least eleven different scents. We're going to need backup."

Benjamin pulled out his cell phone, texted the details to the rest of his squad, and nodded at Thomas to continue. They wandered about the club casually, acting as if they belonged there, trying to get a read on where each of the vampires was located. If they could take them out one at a time they might be able to pull it off, but two against eleven meant they were seriously outnumbered. It didn't help that they were literally surrounded by civilians. The squad's main objective was to do their jobs without the people around them ever knowing about it. Taking on eleven vampires in a single crowded club was not going to help keep their secret.

"I've got three scent trails that lead to the back exit," Thomas said quietly as he turned to head down the dark corridor. Benjamin moved as quickly as he dared. Vampires in the back alley most likely meant they'd already chosen their dinner. At least by confronting their targets outside they wouldn't need to worry about witnesses.

He smelled the blood long before he pushed open the heavy door to the back alley. Despite some of the horrifying things he'd witnessed in his lifetime, the scene was one of the worst he'd ever had to deal with. Just like the reports had warned, the pieces of yet another innocent woman lay strewn all over the alley.

Thomas growled low in his throat, following the scent trails to the end of the alley before doubling back to Benjamin. He shook his head just once, his anger and his grief that they'd gotten here too late to help obvious in every stiff, jerky movement of his limbs.

Benjamin almost didn't notice the blonde woman lying in a crumpled heap between the trash cans. He leaned over to see her face, expecting her to be as dead as the other woman, and nearly dropped to his knees when he realized she still lived.

"Thomas," he called over his shoulder as he lifted the severely injured woman into his arms.

"She's been drained," Thomas said quietly, assessing the situation quickly. "Even if we get her to a hospital, she won't survive. I can already hear the damage to her heart."

Benjamin brushed the tangled blonde hair away from the woman's face and considered doing something he'd never in his lifetime thought he'd do. Thomas must have been thinking along the same lines because he nodded in approval as Benjamin licked the woman's spilled blood from her neck, lifted his own wrist to his mouth, bit into the vein with his incisors, and pressed the warm liquid against the woman's lips.

"Come on, baby girl," Benjamin said under his breath. "Swallow."

* * * *

Samuel entered the club where Benjamin and Thomas had reported at least eleven vampires. It was never a good idea to have so many vamps in the one area, but this small coastal village seemed to have been overrun by them.

He pushed through the gyrating, sweaty humans on the dance floor and followed his squadmate, Alex, to a small group of vampires sitting in the corner. To a human they would have looked like any other group of people in the place, but Samuel and Alex knew better.

And judging by their reaction, the four males and two females recognized who they were also.

The vampire who seemed to be in charge of this little coven stood up and held his hand out with a friendly smile. Sensing no attempt at deception, Samuel took the man's hand and shook it briefly.

"Daniel Seacombe," the man said by way of introduction. "You're the second pair of PUPs in my club tonight. Is there a problem?"

Samuel tried not to take offense to the affectionate nickname, but reducing what he and his squad were to a cute acronym was one of his pet hates. They were members of one of the elite Paranormal Undercover Protection squads, yet the tag made them sound like inexperienced, prepubescent canines. At least their full title, "PUP Squad Alpha," sounded more official. He glanced at Alex, but he showed no signs of having taken offense.

"This is your club?" Samuel asked, trying to get back to the mission.

"Yes, Sir," the vampire said in a deferential voice. "I've owned this little piece of paradise for about forty years now. Fortunately with the ever-changing clientele I haven't found the need to move on."

Samuel nodded. It was one of the biggest problems paranormals faced in the modern world. With the advancements in technology it was getting harder and harder to hide in plain sight. Samuel glanced at his partner, who nodded to his unspoken question, and then explained their presence in the man's club. Their job was to help hide the existence of paranormals from humans, not harass paranormals trying to live peacefully.

"We're currently tracking a paranormal serial killer. Have you seen anyone new in town?"

"It's a tourist town," the guy said with a grimace. "There're always a couple of unknowns in the crowd. I think I counted five earlier but it's been a busy night, and I really didn't have a reason to take too much notice." Samuel nodded. Counting these six, the total number of vampires matched the number Benjamin had texted earlier. "I did see your squadmates heading out the back entrance a few minutes ago. Maybe they noticed something I missed."

"Thanks," Samuel said, handing the man a plain white business card with only a cell phone number on it. "Call that number if you see anything suspicious."

"Of course," the club owner said.

Samuel turned to see that Alex was already heading toward the back of the club. A few moments later they both stepped into the alley.

Benjamin held a pale woman cradled in his arms, his wrist pressed over her mouth as he force-fed the unconscious human his blood.

"Is it working?" Samuel asked as he moved to his friend's side at preternatural speed. It was a surprise to find his best friend trying to make a vampire, but it was obvious by the sickening evidence of violent death around them that she was likely a witness. If they could change her into a vampire and save her life, maybe she'd be able to identify the vamp or vamps who'd done this.

Finally the woman swallowed, her color returning slightly as she began sucking hard against Benjamin's wrist. The man paled, his usual ruddy health suddenly replaced by a sickly, gray pallor. He pulled his wrist away as his knees wobbled, but the woman groaned and immediately lost consciousness.

"She needs too much," Benjamin said breathlessly. "The bastards drained her and left her for dead."

Samuel nodded to his friend's unspoken plea, licked the woman's neck where her blood still spilled, and then bit into his own wrist. He pressed it against the woman's mouth. Almost immediately she began to suck, dragging his life force into her.

After a moment she became less frantic and instead caressed his wrist with her tongue as she drank his blood. Relieved to realize that the woman was going to survive, Samuel finally took a good look at the newly made vampire in his best friend's arms. She wasn't beautiful in a classic sense, but she was very attractive in a wholesome sort of way. It was obvious by her conservative clothes and lack of makeup that she wasn't really part of the nightclub scene they'd just exited.

He touched a finger to her face, smiling when her eyes fluttered open and a look of pure contentment settled on her face. Considering what she'd most likely been through tonight, he hoped that this moment of joy as she began the change from human to vampire would help her through the difficulties to come. Even with the benefit of a couple hundred years' experience, he still found dealing with violent, senseless murders disturbing.

Alex pressed a warm cup filled with human blood into Samuel's hand and handed the other to Benjamin. Samuel smiled gratefully at the club owner hovering by the door. Apparently he catered to more than just the cocktail-swilling humans dancing in his club. Samuel just hoped he was sourcing his human blood legally.

"We'll take care of this," Alex said, glancing around the disturbing scene. It wouldn't do any good to let humans find evidence of the woman's murder. Even if they did figure out what had happened and who had done it, they were unprepared for what they would face if they caught up with the killer. "Take your fledgling back to the motel. We'll meet you there in a couple hours."

Samuel nodded, drained the cup, and handed it back to Alex.

Your fledgling—now there were two words he'd never expected to hear in the same sentence.

* * * *

Skye woke cradled in a man's arms, sucking lazily on the flesh pressed against her lips. Disorientated, she tried to move away, but the man who held her squeezed tighter.

"No," he said in a voice that she wanted to instantly obey, "you need more. Drink, baby girl."

Too tired to argue, Skye swallowed the thick liquid, surprised that she liked the taste. It was salty and had a metallic sort of tang. It was nothing like her usual choice of drink but for some reason seemed like ambrosia sliding down her throat.

She sucked a little longer, caressing the flesh with her tongue as she finally realized the incredible intimacy of her position. She lay cradled against the man's chest, another man's wrist pressed against her mouth, her clothes torn, someone's blood flowing into her, making her stronger, healing her pain.

Blood?

Panicked, she pulled away, wiping her lips with the back of her hand. What the hell was wrong with her? Flashes of what had happened earlier sped through her brain, and she cried out when she remembered the red-haired woman. She tried to lift her head to look around, but the man held her tighter, using his other hand to press her face against his chest.

"You're safe now. Just breathe, baby girl."

"We need to move," another voice said, scaring the hell out of her.

Nearly catatonic with her fear, it was only the fact that both voices were different to those of the men who'd attacked her that allowed her to ask in a raspy voice, "Wh–Who are y–you?"

"It's okay, sweetheart. We're the good guys."

As appealing as it was to lie back and believe the man's reassurance, too many creepy things had happened tonight for her to trust blindly. Swallowing her fear with difficulty, Skye tried once again to look around the area, but the man wouldn't let her lift her head.

"Not now, baby girl," the man said as he started moving.

"The other woman?" she asked without really wanting to know the answer. It was clear by their attackers' behavior that the redhead hadn't been expected to survive.

"I'm sorry," the second man said, his thumb caressing her cheek softly. "We weren't fast enough to save her." Tears flowed freely down Skye's face, as the grief for the terrified young woman overwhelmed all other thoughts. The man simply held her closer and let her cry.

* * * *

Torn between caring for the woman, who was now a fledgling vampire, and needing to salvage their mission, Benjamin looked to Thomas for help. Thomas, the asshole, smiled, shrugged, and then headed back into the club. The rest of their team would have entered the building by now, but unless the other eight vampires inside were involved in this attack as well, it was a good chance that they were simply innocent bystanders. One of them may even be the source of their anonymous tip-off. Without that untraceable e-mail they wouldn't have even been in the area.

The woman was still crying, the sobs softer now, but the grief still very obvious.

Finally conceding to the only course of action possible, Benjamin turned toward the hotel where they were staying and started walking before deciding it was dark enough to use his preternatural speed. Samuel was right beside him.

The young woman was very obviously the victim of a violent attack. With her clothes torn, her neck, shoulders, and hair all covered in blood, and her face streaked with dirt and tears, she was very likely to attract attention. The streets were fairly empty, but he didn't want to chance being stopped by curious pedestrians or maybe even human police, so he used his natural talents to get there as fast as possible.

Once he had the door closed, he glanced around the room and wondered what his next course of action should be. Rescuing damsels in distress wasn't usually part of his mission, and changing said damsel into a vampire had never been part of his plan. He tried to convince himself that his decision had been purely practical—she'd most likely be able to identify her attackers—but a small voice inside called him a liar. His reaction had been based on emotion rather than logic. The other woman's murder had been sickening. His frustration and guilt that they'd been too late meant that he'd eagerly grabbed the chance to save this woman. But he was damned if he'd admit any of that out loud.

"Where?" the woman asked in a tiny voice. She was obviously very tired. Benjamin barely remembered details of his own change so many decades ago, but his sire had told him afterward that he'd pretty much slept for three days and nights straight.

"We're in a hotel room not far from the nightclub where we found you."

"We?" she asked, sounding too tired to be nervous.

"Samuel and me. Thomas and Alex will be here soon. Unless they manage to track down the ones who hurt you, and then I hope they take their sweet time. Did you know the red-haired woman?"

She shook her head, but tears leaked out of her eyes once more. "I–I…I couldn't stop them."

"It's okay, baby girl. There's nothing you could have done."

"Wanted to," she said on a half sob. His heart ached for her. It was likely that her attackers had made it seem she left with them on her own free will. He knew from witness accounts that being compelled by a vampire was a terrifying experience. It was why he used that particular skill very sparingly and then only to nudge a person's natural reaction rather than control it.

Benjamin followed Samuel into the bathroom. They needed to get the woman cleaned up so that they could tuck her into one of the beds and let her sleep, but she seemed in no condition to shower without help. Her eyes were closed and for a moment he was distracted by her pale features. She'd barely had enough blood left for him and Samuel to mix with their own, but it seemed between the two of them they'd managed to complete the process. The ragged wounds on her neck were already beginning to heal.

"Baby girl, your clothes are ripped and covered in blood. We're going to help you get cleaned up." He lowered her feet to the tiled floor and let her lean against him for balance. He glanced at her left hand, glad to notice the absence of a wedding ring. "Can you lift your arms?"

She lifted her arms elbows first, but it was obvious by her soft groan that the action pulled at the wounds at her neck. Making a decision he hoped he wouldn't regret, Benjamin grabbed the collar of her shirt and very carefully tore the material from neck to waist. Samuel pushed the bloodied material down her arms, and Benjamin turned his attention to her pants. They'd been torn in several places and even as he tried to preserve the material he realized that she'd never be able to wear them again. Eventually, he did the same as he'd done to her shirt, tearing the material until it fell away from her.

He'd hoped to be able to at least save her underwear, and thereby her dignity, but the stains had gone right through to her bra and panties.

"What's your name, baby girl?" He probably should have asked much earlier, but there was still a part of him trying to deny the attraction he felt for the pretty blonde. At least by not knowing her name he'd been able to mentally keep an emotional distance between them. Of course the fact that he was one of her sires meant that they were already connected. Still, it seemed appropriate to ask the woman's name before suggesting she allow him to remove her underwear.

She was very tired, and maybe hiding her embarrassment behind it, but she managed to mumble "Skye Hastings" without actually opening her eyes.

"Well, Skye Hastings, I wish we'd met under better circumstances, but I was hoping it would be okay to remove your underwear before we step into the shower."

* * * *

Before *we* step into the shower? We?

The meaning of that sentence finally penetrated the fog in Skye's brain and she forced herself to open her eyes and look around. The fact that she was already down to her underwear was a little disconcerting, but it was the dirty, smelly, blood-stained state of the clothing that hit her hardest.

She glanced at what was once a soft, purple lace trim on her bra and shuddered in revulsion. She'd always hated blood, but finding herself covered in it was pretty much her worst nightmare. Maybe it was the years she'd spent working as a receptionist for a doctor, but she had an almost obsessive aversion to the stuff. Without giving any thought to the stranger holding her up or the one standing beside her, she reached behind her back, undid the clasp and dropped the material to the ground. A quick glance at her panties, and they hit the floor as well. She turned to the shower without consciously noticing that she was in an unfamiliar bathroom, but felt her knees give out as she tried to step into the stall.

"Whoa, baby girl, hold on for just one more minute."

She growled her annoyance at the delay but sagged gratefully in the other man's hold as he set the water running and then helped her stand under the spray. The first man stepped in behind her, pulling her close as he washed away the putrid feeling. She sighed as he angled her head under the spray and tipped a sweet-smelling shampoo into her hair.

Skye held on to the waistband of his soaked pants as he massaged the fragrant bubbles through her hair. When he'd rinsed and then combed conditioner through her hair, he grabbed the shower gel and cleaned her all over. She felt his body react when he cleaned her more private areas, but he washed her quickly and efficiently without acknowledging his body's needs.

Clean and smelling far more pleasant, Skye let him wrap her in a towel and lift her into the other man's arms. The first guy quickly shredded his own wet clothing, wrapped a towel around his waist, and followed her and the other guy into the main room.

She smiled sleepily as the one holding her pulled back the blankets on one of the beds and tucked her in. None of it seemed real—not the shower, the dark alley, the men who'd attacked her, the woman who'd died so quietly… Panic streaked through her and she reached for his hand as he went to move away.

"Please, stay with me," she begged, terrified that everything she remembered was true.

"It's okay, Skye. I'm not going anywhere. I'll just be right over there."

"Please," she asked again. She winced at the needy sound in her voice but figured if there was ever a situation that warranted a certain amount of pleading, this was it.

"I need to get cleaned up," he said, looking down at the blood on his hands. He glanced at his friend and raised an eyebrow in silent question. The guy wrapped in a towel seemed to hesitate, and it didn't even occur to her that she didn't know his name until he nodded his head and climbed onto the mattress beside her. Staying above the blankets, the man curled his body protectively around hers and held her close.

Before she could think of a polite way to ask an almost-naked stranger lying in bed with her what his name was, the need for sleep took her voice. Barely conscious she felt the other man lean over her for a moment before he pressed a soft kiss to her forehead and moved away.

Feeling safe and protected for the first time that night, Skye went gratefully into the warm, dark abyss of deep sleep.

Chapter Two

Benjamin held the woman close, trying to deny the unexpected attraction. It was true that he'd been a long time without a female to warm his bed, but still his body's unconscious response seemed inappropriate. She was a witness to murder. And a fledgling vampire. Her life was about to kaleidoscope in ways she'd probably never imagined possible.

Modern humans didn't even believe in vampires or werewolves. How was Skye Hastings going to cope when she found out that they not only existed but that she was now one of them?

He heard Thomas's distinctive footsteps long before the man used his keycard to enter the room.

"How is she?" Thomas whispered even though the sound was quite loud to vampire ears.

"Tired, frightened, and finally asleep."

"Was she able to give you a description of the vamps who attacked her?"

Benjamin smiled at his friend's impatience. "No, the change takes time. She's likely to do nothing but sleep and eat for several days." Obviously Thomas knew even less about making someone a vampire than Benjamin did. The fact that Skye was now, according to sacred vampire tradition, his and Samuel's responsibility until she was capable of existing by herself added a complication Benjamin wasn't certain he was prepared to deal with. He'd spent the last ten minutes mentally selecting and then discarding every vampire he knew who could possibly take over Skye's lessons in Vampire 101. Unfortunately, it seemed when it came to fledgling vampires the urge to protect them overrode all other considerations. It seemed the accepted "law" that the maker was responsible for the new vampire was more of a physical compulsion than an actual rule in their society.

Thomas sat down tiredly, his need to catch the vampires responsible for these horrific attacks obviously weighing on him heavily. They'd worked together for more than five decades, and if Benjamin knew anything about his werewolf partner, it was that he didn't like losing—ever.

"Their trail stopped about four blocks from the nightclub. It dead-ended at a parking lot, so we're pretty sure they're using modern forms of transportation." Benjamin almost smiled at his partner's dislike of cars. Born during a time when life moved much more slowly, Thomas had never made a secret of his dislike for vehicles that could travel faster than a horse. Apparently his distaste extended all the way to the word "car."

Fortunately, Thomas was also a soldier who knew that modern transportation was a necessary evil that, over long distances, enabled them to do their jobs properly. Benjamin had overheard Thomas's whispered self-pep talk more than once—"I don't have to like it. I just have to do it."

"So where do we go from here?" Benjamin asked. Technically, he was the commanding officer of their PUP squad but they'd all been working together so long that every man knew the strengths and weaknesses of each of his teammates as well as he knew his own. These days they worked together like a well-oiled machine. It was very rare that Benjamin had to do more than agree with his team's suggestions.

"Wilson has been trying to trace the e-mail back to its origin but whoever sent it knows an awful lot about tech. Maybe even more than Wilson." Benjamin raised an eyebrow, laughing softly as Thomas added, "And if you tell him I said that you are going to be one very unhappy vampire."

It was no secret that Wilson considered himself one of the world's leading hackers. Fortunately for their PUP squad he was probably right. It sure wouldn't sit well with him to come across a puzzle he couldn't break, and knowing Wilson, he'd probably remain hunched over his keyboard doing whatever it was he did until he had an answer.

"What about the club? Did anyone see Skye or the other woman leave?"

"None that we could find. Alex tried the concerned-big-brother routine but all he got was adoring fans wanting to give him their numbers." Even after fifty years of working together, Benjamin still couldn't believe how easily Alex attracted women. They practically fell at his feet wherever he went. "The club owner identified us straight away. He seemed friendly enough, but I reckon he's probably given every paranormal living in town the heads-up as to our presence."

"It shouldn't be too much of a problem. The vamps we're looking for are unlikely to be locals. They're probably just passing through." He glanced down at the woman sleeping in his arms. "With a bit of luck the locals will close ranks and protect their town from any unknowns. Did you manage to control the murder scene?"

Thomas looked a little offended by the question. Normally Benjamin was working right beside him on cases like this, and if the woman in his arms hadn't been in such dire need, this mission would have been like any other.

"Again," Thomas said on an exhaled breath, "I'm pretty sure every local member of the paranormal community will know all about it by morning, but the humans and their law enforcement should remain unaware. Alex put in a call for a pixie cleaning crew." Thomas shuddered as he said the last three words. Pixies were well known in the paranormal world as assassins for hire but were often engaged by the Ruling Body to help hide evidence of violent death from humans. The cleaning crews were very good at their job. It was the fact that they looked like seven-year-old human girls that gave Benjamin and the rest of his team the creeps.

Skye rolled in his arms, wriggling closer as she continued to sleep. Absently he ran his hand over her hair, soothing her as he continued his conversation with Thomas.

"Tomorrow," Thomas said with a slightly amused smile as he glanced at what Benjamin was doing with his hand, "Alex and I are planning to talk to some of the locals. There are quite a few businesses in town owned by paranormals. If the women's attackers have money they'll probably be staying in one of the motels. Maybe one of the locals took notice." He shrugged. At this point in their mission they inevitably hit a few dead ends. "If not, we'll check into some of the more common vamp hidey-holes in the afternoon." Thomas's tone of voice suggested he wasn't looking forward to going wandering through the underground sewers. With his keen sense of smell it was bound to be unpleasant, but Benjamin knew his team well enough to know that they would all do what needed to be done when it needed to be done.

In years gone by Benjamin would have suggested his friend plan to get some sleep also, but experience had taught him that when Thomas felt this strongly about a case that he should be left to do his job.

"What about Skye?" Thomas asked with an expression Benjamin couldn't really classify. "Should we consider you and Samuel off the mission for the moment?"

"Maybe," Benjamin said as Samuel stepped through the door adjoining the two hotel rooms. "We can't leave her unprotected. If her attackers think she can identify them, she could be in even more danger." Samuel nodded in agreement. It was most likely that he'd been listening to the conversation from the other room anyway. Vampire hearing might not be as good as a werewolf's, but it was still way better than when they'd been human.

"And the Ruling Body would be all over us if we left a fledgling to her own devices. There's no telling what she might do if she wakes alone," Samuel added.

Benjamin hadn't even thought of that. For at least the next couple of days Skye's actions were likely to be ruled by instinct rather than her adult mind. It was probably the main reason why the Ruling Body had chosen to put a maker's natural inclination to protect a fledgling vampire into their written laws. Protecting the secret of the paranormal community's existence was essentially the reason they had a Ruling Body in the first place. Fledgling vampires could wreak all sorts of havoc if left to their own devices, and they certainly wouldn't be aware of how their actions affected the rest of the paranormal community. Human beings as a whole tended to react poorly to things they didn't understand and if history had taught Benjamin anything, it was that very few humans could be trusted to react calmly and rationally upon discovering that creatures supposedly only found in nightmares actually existed.

There was a good chance that Skye wasn't going to take the news of her change very well either.

Thomas glanced at Samuel and then back at Benjamin. "I'm going to go bunk in with Alex. It'll make it easier for you two to care for Skye if you're sharing the same room."

Benjamin nodded his thanks, and within minutes Thomas had collected his stuff and moved into the adjoining room. Samuel sat down in the chair Thomas had vacated and, as if he couldn't help himself, leaned over and ran his fingers through the silky strands of Skye's long, straight, blonde hair.

"I've drafted a report for Higgins, I'm not quite sure how to phrase 'Oh and we made a vampire,' so I sort of left it out."

"It's probably not something the Ruling Body needs to know. What we do on our own time is our business. If Skye is able to identify her attackers we'll explain her transformation then."

Samuel sat back, letting Skye's hair fall onto the bed. "I didn't expect the attraction to be so strong," he said quietly.

"I know what you mean," Benjamin said as he tried to move so that his hard cock wasn't pressed against Skye's hip.

"Do you think it was like this for our maker?"

Benjamin smiled at the man who'd once been his cousin. As humans they'd grown up together, gone to school together, fought in war together, and then died together. They'd been reborn as vampires when a man had found them in the middle of a bloody battlefield, their lives ebbing away so very slowly that Benjamin remembered most of the thoughts that had gone through his mind that day.

"It might explain Elijah's rush to leave us behind." In fact it explained a lot of things that had happened back then. Despite their sire's seemingly callous need to teach them quickly and send them on their way, they had both sensed that Elijah was a loving and generous man. He'd been devastated as he'd weaved his way through the battlefield seeking survivors. When he'd found them, he'd risked his own life by turning two humans at once. If they'd been as close to death as Skye had, they would certainly have killed him with their need for vampire blood.

"Makes me kind of glad that Skye was the first human we changed. I think I'd probably freak out if I felt this sort of attraction for a male fledgling."

"Me, too," Benjamin said, watching his friend closely. "But the one thing Elijah proved is that we don't have to follow through on it. He walked away. Once Skye is capable of taking care of herself we should be able to walk away, too."

A flash of anger filled Samuel's face, but it was gone almost immediately. He seemed to hesitate, as if he were going to say something else, but then he nodded once and sat back in the chair.

* * * *

Samuel woke suddenly, his hearing quickly zeroing in on the sound that had roused him. The sun was due to rise in the next few hours. Thanks to his advanced age he no longer felt the physical drain and need for sleep, but their beautiful fledgling would fall into a deep slumber as soon as the first rays lightened the sky on the horizon.

But for the moment she whimpered, caught inside a nightmare she couldn't wake from.

Benjamin had reluctantly dragged himself out of bed a few hours ago and gone to confer with the rest of PUP Squad Alpha. Samuel had made the somewhat sensible decision to watch over Skye from the chair beside the bed—despite the nearly overwhelming urge to wrap himself around the beautiful blonde and hold on tight.

He leaned over and gently shook her. "Skye, wake up, sweetheart."

She partially opened her eyes, but the look of panic that crossed her features seemed to be from something only she could see. "No!" she screamed almost silently.

"Skye," Samuel said a little more forcefully. Her eyes flew open, but this time she seemed to recognize him and scrambled into his embrace instead.

Shocked by the unexpected move, Samuel almost pushed her away as thoughts of his own self-preservation surfaced. Despite his attraction to her, it was best for all involved if he and Benjamin kept a professional and emotional distance. She was witness to a vicious murder. Nothing more.

But the internal pep talk did nothing to stop his arms from closing around her and holding her tight. Completely naked, she snuggled against him, her fear already dissipating as she once again fell asleep. He held her close as he tried to rationalize his feelings, but it was several long minutes before he realized that she'd instinctively trusted him. Whatever else was going on inside her mind, Skye felt a connection to him, just as he felt one to her.

Chapter Three

Skye woke lying in the embrace of a stranger.

No, not a stranger. Not really. But rather someone she knew but hadn't really met.

Not that any of that made a lick of sense.

"Good morning, sweetheart," the man said as she nuzzled her face against his neck. She had an insane urge to lick him all over. Considering all the hard muscles he seemed to own, that probably wasn't so surprising, but it was the fact that she couldn't remember where they met or how she ended up sleeping in his arms that stopped her from following through.

"Good morning," she mumbled, trying to look around the room they were in. "Where are we?"

"The motel on the corner of Main and Ocean Streets."

"Oh," she said, trying to hide her embarrassment. She supposed it could be worse. If she was going to tumble into bed with a complete stranger at least she'd picked one with money enough for a decent room. Although sex with a stranger sure wasn't her usual style.

Movement on the bed behind her had the hair on the back of her neck standing up in fear, and a quick glance over her shoulder confirmed that there was indeed a man lying on the mattress. Hell, did she have sex with two strangers last night?

"Um..." She wasn't a big drinker, so she couldn't quite fathom how she'd gotten here. The worst-case scenario slipped into her head, but it didn't seem wise to accuse two very large men of drugging her until she had some idea of how she would get out of here. The guy on the bed seemed to read her predicament because he rolled to his feet, pulled on a pair of jeans, and dragged a seat closer to where she sat on the other guy's lap.

"I'm Benjamin," he said. "The guy holding you is Samuel. Do you remember anything that happened?"

She shook her head.

"You were attacked in the alley behind the nightclub on the beach."

"I was?" It was probably very foolish, but something inside her urged her to trust these men. "Did I hit my head? I don't remember anything at all."

She'd had some crazy dreams that proved she watched way too much television, but she didn't have any memory of leaving the club. Why would she even go into the back alley? Her sister had arranged to meet her inside, and Skye distinctly remembered going in the front door.

"Jennifer," she said quickly, levering herself off the man's lap in search of a phone. "What time is it? Knowing my sister she's probably filed a missing person's report by now."

"Skye, we'll call your sister in a little while, but first we need to explain what happened to you."

She held up her hands in a physical effort to halt his words. "Look, if it's all the same to you, I'd rather live in blissful ignorance. I don't remember what happened, and quite frankly, judging by your serious faces, I'd rather not know. I have weird enough dreams as it is without adding real-life experiences into the mix." Both men looked annoyed at her announcement, but it was the fact that they seemed to be trying very hard to keep their eyes on her face that finally tipped her into noticing she was standing in front of them naked. With a squeak of embarrassment she snatched the sheet off Samuel's knees and wrapped it around herself. "What happened to my clothes?"

"They were damaged beyond repair so we threw them out."

She paced back and forth as she tried to comprehend what was going on but somehow still retain the ignorance that she suspected was keeping her sane. Something inside warned her that she really, *really* didn't want to remember anything about last night.

"So if I can just call my sister, she can...um...bring me some clothes and I'll get out of your hair."

"Skye," Benjamin said with very sincere-sounding sympathy in his voice, "I know it would be much easier to forget everything that happened, but you're our only living witness to a young woman's murder. And there are things that we need to explain about what happened after you were attacked."

Oh crap. If he was about to tell her that the three of them all had wild monkey sex afterward, she wasn't sure she wanted to hear that either.

"Look, it's fine. I'm on the pill. Whatever happened I'm sure we all, you know, enjoyed it, so there's no need to go through a...um...blow-by-blow description." She winced as soon as the words were out of her mouth—the pun truly had not been intended—but she was too embarrassed to look over and see their faces.

But then Benjamin was somehow standing in front of her, even though she hadn't actually noticed him move.

"We didn't have sex, baby girl," he said even though he touched her face with the familiarity of a lover. "You were dying when we found you, so we did the one thing we knew to save you."

"Dying?" she asked in disbelief. If she'd been dying, why wasn't she in a hospital?

"Sweetheart," Samuel said as he, too, moved to stand in front of her, "if there had been any other choice, we wouldn't have done it."

"Done what?" she asked suspiciously as flashes of memory played behind her eyes. Fear gripped her as the face of a frightened woman floated through her mind.

"They'd drained you, Skye. We had no choice but to change you into a vampire."

Vampire? She wanted to laugh hysterically, but in her heart she knew their words were true. Even now the memories she'd tried to deny only minutes earlier rose up to suffocate her.

"The woman with red hair?" she asked, already knowing the answer.

"I'm sorry, sweetheart," Samuel said as he pulled her into his arms. She went willingly, overwhelmed by everything that had happened in that dark alley. When her attackers—she'd known even then that they'd been vampires who'd bitten her—had dropped her between the trash cans, she'd known she would die.

But then the incongruity of the situation finally hit her.

"Vampires tried to kill me, and then you guys saved me by turning me into a vampire? Are you vampires, too?"

With her ear pressed against Samuel's chest she could hear the man's heart beating. How could he be a vampire? Weren't vampires considered the *un*dead? But her disbelief was quickly quelled by Benjamin's reply.

"Yes, baby girl, we're vampires." He reached over and pushed a stray lock of hair behind her ear. Too late she realized it was so he could see her face more clearly. "And since we made you, we're responsible for teaching you how to survive your new life."

"So you're going to teach me how to…what? Kill humans?"

Benjamin ran a hand down his face in obvious agitation. "We don't kill humans to feed. It's not necessary. Even before blood banks it wasn't necessary to kill humans to survive."

"Sweetheart," Samuel said as he shuffled her back toward the bed, "we know it's a lot to take in when you're still so tired, but we really need your help to track down your attackers. Do you remember anything at all about last night?"

She shook her head, trying to dislodge the images beating through her brain. She didn't want to remember, but the fear on the woman's face before she'd died lodged front and center in her memory, and Skye knew she was being a coward. She was safe now. How she knew that she wasn't quite sure—these men were strangers, mostly—but her heart told her they would lay their own lives down in an effort to protect her.

"The man...the vampire who killed her...he wasn't very tall. His hair was blond and sort of scraggly...dirty looking."

"How many vampires were there?"

"Th–Three." She swallowed heavily as memories of staring at the night sky, as the two vampires drained her of blood, crowded her brain.

"Do you remember what the other two looked like?" Samuel asked as he guided her onto the mattress and helped her to lie down. He lay down behind her, holding her close as tears rolled down her cheeks. Benjamin sat in front of her, the concern on his face very obvious as she haltingly described the two men who'd taken her out of the club against her will.

"H–How did they make me do that?"

"It's a skill all vampires have. We can compel humans, but it's something we try to avoid. It can be very frightening for the human." She nodded in agreement. It had been beyond terrifying to not have any control over her own actions. Samuel rubbed a thumb over her stomach where his hand rested, the gentle touch quite comforting.

"Are you hungry?" Benjamin asked. She gave him a watery smile. It was obvious he didn't want to frighten her by dredging up too many memories. Unfortunately, the entire experience was replaying in her brain. She hoped that maybe if she told them everything, it would help lessen the memory's impact.

By the time she was finished talking, her voice was hoarse, her eyes felt swollen and raw, and her chest ached with grief, but a very small part of her knew it was the first step to reclaiming her life.

"Thank you, Skye," Benjamin said as he leaned over and pressed a kiss to her forehead. "You're an amazing young woman." He glanced at the interconnecting door, and she finally noticed two more men standing just outside the room. The new faces probably should have frightened her, but she was too exhausted to feel much of anything.

One of the men stepped into the room, reached into the small fridge, and lifted out what seemed to be a bag of blood. She shuddered in revulsion as he poured some into a coffee mug and brought it over to her.

Her mouth watered at the appealing smell, but her brain clung to fears she'd learned while working in the medical industry. Samuel reached over and took the cup when Skye refused to reach for it. She wanted to back away from the mug full of biohazard waste, but with Samuel behind her she had nowhere to go.

The man who'd stayed in the doorway smiled kindly at her reaction. "You'll get used to it. I don't know all that much about newly made vampires but I do know you need blood to survive."

Skye nodded even though the thought of drinking blood made her stomach twist in an anxious knot. "Are you..."

She didn't manage to get the whole sentence out, but it was obvious by the man's next words that he'd known what she was going to ask. "Nope, Alex and I—I'm Thomas, by the way—aren't vampires. I'm a werewolf." He glanced at the man he'd identified as Alex, gave a mischievous sort of grin, and added, "Alex is something else."

"Oh," she said, not really ready for any more surprises. She'd gone from blissful ignorance to suddenly learning that vampires and werewolves really did exist. She didn't even want to know what "something else" meant.

Again Thomas seemed to understand, because he glanced at Benjamin and Samuel, nodded to Alex, and then the two men left the room.

"You need to drink this, sweetheart," Samuel said as he held the cup closer to her face.

"I don't think I can. You know—AIDS, hepatitis, deadly diseases that kill innocent people..."

Benjamin seemed to smile at that. "Skye, you're no longer 'people.' You're a vampire now. Blood-borne diseases like that only taint the taste of the blood. They can't hurt you. Not anymore."

"Oh." It was turning out to be a rather weird conversation. Even though inside her head she knew they were telling her the truth, she couldn't quite extend her belief to the fact that she would now need to drink blood to survive. "Um…maybe later."

Benjamin gave her a look that told her he knew she was stalling, but he stepped closer, took the mug from Samuel, and placed it on the bedside table where she could reach it.

"Can I call my sister now? What time is it? She must beside herself with worry."

"Sure," Samuel said as his arm tightened around her middle for a moment, "as soon as we figure out what you should tell her. The whole vampire part is something best left out." Benjamin nodded in agreement and then helped her to her feet. This time she managed to take the sheet with her.

"So what should I tell her?"

Samuel shrugged. "It's been our experience that trying to hold on to the life you had while human just makes everything more complicated. You can't tell her about being a vampire. You can't go out in the sunshine. You'll always feel cold to a human's touch. You'll be faster and stronger than you ever thought possible, but none of that is compatible with your old life. I'm sorry, Skye, but life as you knew it is over." He stepped closer, touching her face even though he seemed to try not to. "Technically you would have died last night so your sister would have lost you anyway."

"So I shouldn't call my sister?" That didn't sit well with Skye at all. Jennifer had spent her entire life taking her role as big sister very seriously. To disappear without a trace seemed beyond cruel.

Benjamin handed her a cell phone. "Call her. Tell her you're leaving town for a few days. We'll figure out the rest later."

"I'm leaving town?" Yesterday she was a boring doctor's receptionist whose idea of a good time was to read a book in bed. Her sister wasn't going to believe that she just decided to take a holiday without saving and planning and booking everything in advance. She wasn't a fly-by-the-seat-of-her-pants type of person.

"Tell her you met a man," Samuel suggested with a wink. Technically she'd met two men if the way they both kept touching her meant anything, but that was probably an even more unlikely scenario from her sister's point of view. "Trust me," he said.

She rolled her eyes at his exaggerated lascivious expression but smiled at his attempt at humor. Her emotions were all over the place, so it was kind of nice to have Benjamin's solid practicality and Samuel's light humor to keep her grounded.

Skye took the phone, dialed her sister's number, and winced at the overly loud greeting from her sister. Jennifer's voice was hoarse, her tone hopeful, but it was her reaction to Skye's first word that broke her heart.

"Oh, thank God. Skye, honey, I've been so worried. Are you okay? Do you need a lift? Where are you? I'll come get you."

"Jen, I'm okay. I just…lost track of time."

"That's okay," Jennifer said quickly. Obviously she was very upset to accept such a vague excuse. "Just tell me where you are and I'll come get you. The important thing is that we get you home where you're safe."

"Jen," Skye said. She shot Benjamin a pleading look. She just wanted to tell her sister she'd come home straight away. He gave her a sympathetic look but shook his head slightly. "Jen, I…um…met a man. He…um…we…um…we're going to…"

Samuel leaned over and grabbed the phone from her. Ordinarily she'd be appalled at any man who tried to interfere in a conversation between her and her sister, but today she was grateful. Maybe Samuel would be able to soothe her sister's worries.

"Hi, Jennifer. This is Samuel Eldridge. I feel I must apologize for monopolizing your sister's time. We very literally talked all night. We were only supposed to sleep for a little while, but before we knew it the day was over."

The day was over? Skye moved toward the window and peeked out the blind to see that night had indeed fallen. She must have slept nearly twenty hours. Was it any wonder her sister was frantic with worry?

Samuel continued talking to Jennifer, charming her into believing that Skye had really chosen to take an unplanned holiday on a whirlwind romance. Surprisingly, Samuel rattled off a cell phone number and assured her sister that she could call Skye at any time. It obviously went a long way to convincing Jennifer to trust him because he handed the phone back to her a moment later.

"Jen?"

"Skye, he sounds like a decent guy. Are you sure about this? I mean, don't let him charm you into something you don't really want to do. If you really don't want to go with him, tell me where you are and I'll come get you." Apparently, Samuel wasn't quite as convincing as he thought he was.

"No, Jen. I'm happy to go with him. I need this." Technically she was referring to the time it would take to adjust to living in the paranormal world, but her sister took it the way she'd hoped.

"You do. You really do. It's about time you had some excitement in your life."

"Thanks, Jen. I'll call you when I can."

"Damn straight you will, or I'll track you and lover boy down." The words were affectionately spoken, but Skye had no doubt her sister meant every word. She smiled at Jennifer's ability to always support her, the grin widening as her overprotective, wonderfully loving big sister started rattling off the practicalities. "I'll call your boss and let him know you're taking time off. With the amount of vacation time he owes you he has no right to complain at the short notice. I'll keep an eye on your place. Water the plants. Collect your mail. Have I forgotten anything?"

"I don't think so," Skye said with a smile in her voice.

"Okay, well, have fun. Call me. And for heaven's sake use a condom."

Judging by the smirks covering both men's faces, they could hear both sides of this conversation.

"Of course," she said, trying not to look at the blood slowly congealing in a coffee cup not five feet away from her. "Thanks, Jen. I'm really glad you're my sister."

"Back at you, kid," she said in echo of their teenage years. There was only a four-year gap between them, but when Jennifer had been sixteen and Skye only twelve, it had seemed insurmountable. These days they were very literally best friends.

Sighing with relief that at least her sister wasn't worrying herself to death, Skye turned to the men and waited for one of them to tell her what would happen next.

"You know we don't need condoms, right?"

She smiled at Samuel's take on what was most important from that conversation.

"So, now what?"

"Now you feed and get some more sleep."

It wasn't until he said the words that she realized just how tired she really was. Hell, she'd slept practically a whole day, how could she still be sleepy?

"It's the change, sweetheart," Samuel said as he lifted her in his arms and carried her back to the bed. "You'll likely sleep for a few more days yet, but when the change is complete, you'll notice an increase in hearing and visual acuity. You'll be stronger and able to move much faster than before. You won't be able to walk in the sun without completely covering every inch of skin, but there are considerable advantages to being a vampire."

"But before you can do any of that, you need to feed," Benjamin said as he held the cup of blood out to her. He frowned when she shook her head. "Skye, if you leave it too long between feeds you're likely to go sucking on some poor innocent passerby. Part of what we need to teach you is how to control your hunger."

"I'm fine. I'm not hungry, really."

"If you say so," Benjamin said with what could only be described as fake nonchalance. He slid onto the bed beside her and pressed a soft kiss to her lips. Unexpectedly he deepened the contact, groaning as his tongue slid into her open mouth and explored inside. She sighed as Samuel lay down behind her, his hands traveling over her hip and thigh, gliding higher to skim over her breast, the nipple pulling tight, demanding more. She was panting, her body alive with arousal, her pussy leaking juices onto her thighs as they both suddenly stopped.

Benjamin held her close, pressing her face against his throat as she tried to comprehend why they'd stopped. But then the delicious smell of the blood pounding through the vein in his neck caught her attention, and before she understood what she intended, she sank her teeth into his flesh.

He groaned, pulling her over the top of him as she fed. He tore impatiently at the material of the sheet, finally untangling it so that he could spread her naked body over his. She could feel his hard cock pressed against the entrance to her pussy. He tilted his hips, pushing her hard against his denim-covered erection.

She swallowed his blood, moaning at the delicious taste, sucking harder as orgasm spun closer.

But then his large hand was there, pulling her away from his throat, the delicious taste of his life-blood taken from her before either of her hungers were sated.

He slid out from under her, grabbed the cup of blood, and handed it to her. This time she took it, confused by her own actions, bewildered by his behavior, and supremely pissed off to be denied something she'd wanted so much.

"Drink, baby girl," he said in a voice that showed he was hurting as much as her right now.

She tipped the cup into her mouth, pleasantly surprised that the cold human blood didn't taste nearly as bad as she'd been expecting. She drained it and handed him back the empty cup.

"Get some rest," Benjamin said, touching her face affectionately as Samuel pulled her into the cradle of his body and got them both comfortable. She wanted to deny her need for sleep and demand they give her body the release she'd been craving, but an unexpected wave of dizziness overtook her, and she felt her eyelids shut.

Chapter Four

"That was cruel," Samuel said with a soft laugh, caressing his hand through Skye's hair as the beautiful blonde fell asleep.

"She had to experience firsthand what it was like to lose control if she didn't feed. It was the only way I could think of to show her safely."

"Oh, I have no objections to the lesson, just the part where *I'm* lying here aching."

Benjamin grimaced. "You think you're aching. When she bit me…" He let the words trail off as he ran a hand through his hair. "I never expected the experience to be quite so erotic. I meant only to show her what happened when she loses control. *My* desperate need for *her* wasn't actually something I anticipated."

"I know what you mean," Samuel said as he tried to adjust his jeans to a more comfortable position.

Benjamin sat on the edge of the bed and stared at Skye's face, now relaxed in sleep. "It would seem that when it comes to our newly made vampire, neither of us has the willpower we once had."

"So what are we going to do about it?" Samuel asked the question in a light tone of voice, but it seemed by his friend's reaction that Benjamin wasn't fooled. It was obvious that they were both very attracted to the beautiful blonde.

"I'm not sure," Benjamin said slowly. "She seems to feel an attraction to both of us as well, but that could just be a reaction to the change. Not many humans are open-minded enough to enter a triad relationship."

"Is that what you want?" Samuel asked, trying not to sound too eager. They'd shared the last two hundred years side by side. It almost seemed appropriate that they would share a woman as well.

"I don't think it matters what we want," Benjamin said, leaning over and smoothing hair away from Skye's face. "It's up to Skye."

* * * *

Thank heaven for e-readers.

Skye would have been bored out of her skull if Samuel hadn't been able to retrieve her favorite piece of technology from her apartment. He'd also gathered clothes, shoes, and toiletries so that she would feel more comfortable surrounded by her own stuff as she slowly changed into a vampire.

She'd met the whole squad—all ten members in the past few days. She'd been overwhelmed with how many different paranormal species they represented, but had been assured that being surrounded by werewolves, bear-shifters, demons, warlocks, and of course other vampires, would eventually feel normal. For now, they all treated her like a little sister. She didn't mind it so much from the others, but from Samuel and Benjamin it was quite annoying.

They'd spent the last three nights on the road, tracking the movements of the vampires who'd attacked her. Of course, Skye had spent most of that time sleeping, but the awake hours were becoming increasingly frustrating. Each morning Benjamin crawled into the bed with her, held her close, and admonished her to get some sleep, and each evening she woke curled in Samuel's embrace. Neither man seemed inclined to pursue any type of physical relationship. Anytime she considered throwing herself at one or both of them, memories of the bite she'd taken out of Benjamin rose up to haunt her. She'd never experienced anything quite so erotic in her life—well, her human life, at least. It had made her more cautious about feeding when they said she should, but it hadn't quelled the need building inside her. Each night things became just that much harder.

Now that she didn't require as much sleep, Skye was noticing all the changes becoming a vampire had wrought on her body. Just as they'd told her it would, her eyesight and hearing had improved immensely. She was stronger, faster, and way more coordinated than she'd ever been in her human life. The trouble was that it also made her incredibly more sensitive to touch.

She had no idea if that was normal for a vampire or not, but she found herself buying increasingly erotic romances on her e-reader and devouring them in mere hours. Thank heavens it was all electronic. If she'd actually had to go into a store and buy the books, she would have been mortified by the thought that they might see. As it was, she was having a hard time hiding the effects the stories were having on her.

"Not tired?" Benjamin asked as he stepped through the adjoining door between this motel room and the one Alex and Thomas were sharing. As far as she could tell, that was fairly standard practice for the ten members of their PUP squad. She'd almost giggled when she'd heard the acronym, yet it was obvious that not only did they do an important job, but that they were all very good at it.

"No," Skye said shyly. That was the weirdest part. Despite the fact that she was wildly attracted to both of these men, the more she got to know them, the quieter she'd become. A part of her wondered if that was why neither man had kissed her since that night. Unless it was because she'd hurt Benjamin by feeding on him. The question was out of her mouth before she'd really decided to ask it.

He looked surprised. "No, baby girl, you didn't hurt me."

"So why haven't you...I mean why...um..." It was obvious that he was following precisely what she meant even though her ability to verbalize her thoughts wasn't exactly working.

He leaned over and cupped her face in his warm hand. Funny how a few days ago he'd seemed cold to her touch. Would she now feel as cold to another human as he once had to her? He smiled slightly, but seemed to hesitate before speaking.

"The change can be traumatic and confusing. We just didn't want to make it worse."

"So you do want to kiss me?"

He smiled, whispered the words "of course," but then moved away instead of moving closer.

"So why don't you?" She could feel her cheeks turning bright red with her embarrassment. It seemed that was something becoming a vampire hadn't changed.

"Because I want to kiss you, too," Samuel said from the doorway.

"So you're...um...waiting for me to choose, or something?"

Benjamin shrugged, but Samuel was more direct. He walked over to the chair where she sat, lifted her to her feet, and pulled her into his embrace. She went happily. It felt right to let him hold her—to let them both hold her—and she didn't want to be denied that closeness any longer.

"We didn't want to overwhelm you."

"Uh-huh." It probably sounded a little sarcastic, and maybe it was, but being kissed by two men she was attracted to seemed the least overwhelming of the things that had happened in the past week.

Samuel laughed as if he could hear every word in her head. "So, should I take it that you're comfortable kissing both of us?"

Again embarrassment heated her cheeks, but she reminded herself that she'd spent her human years "playing it safe" and all it had done was make her lonely. Maybe her new life as a vampire was a chance to embrace the things she wanted. She nodded, determined to brazen out the red-faced embarrassment.

"What about," Benjamin asked as he moved closer and embraced her from behind, "kissing both of us at the same time?"

"I think that m–might be a little d–difficult from a logistical point of view." Her words may have stumbled, but it wasn't from fear. Heat was already swirling through her body as images of the ménage stories she'd been reading danced through her mind.

"True," Samuel said with another soft laugh as he slid his hands to the front of her shirt and gently massaged her aching breasts through the material. "How would you feel about kissing me while Benjamin fucks you?"

"I–I–I"—*Wow, did it just get way hotter in here?*—"think I might enjoy that," she said as her body tightened and throbbed in response to his naughty words. Benjamin groaned and pulled her tightly against his body, his hard cock pressing against the crease of her ass. Samuel took her lips in a devastating kiss, his tongue exploring her mouth with a desperation that thrilled her. Finally, he pulled away, panting hard.

"Tell us to stop," Benjamin whispered in her ear as his hands caressed her stomach through the thin material of her shirt.

"No," she answered on a whimper, not sure if she was begging them to continue or demanding that they hurry up. "Please *don't* stop."

"Good girl," Samuel said as he turned her around so that Benjamin could press fiery kisses all over her face, his hands exploring every newly naked inch of her as Samuel stripped her clothing away. They laid her down on the bed, her body aching with need, her pussy swollen and dripping with her desire. She watched them quickly undress, panting harder when she realized their beautifully sculpted bodies weren't just a trick of the clothing they wore. Both men were lean and muscular, perfectly shaped.

Benjamin slid onto the bed, his hard cock pressed up against her thigh as he took her mouth again, this time thrusting his tongue deep, mimicking the act they all wanted. Samuel crawled onto the bed, wedging his knees between hers, forcing her thighs wide open. He touched her pussy with his fingers, gently caressing the swollen folds for a moment before dropping his head and pressing a kiss to her clit.

Heat surged through her, the gentle touch more arousing than anything she could remember experiencing as a human. She lifted her hips, opening her legs wider, begging with her body for more. Samuel's tongue flicked over her flesh, licking and laving her swollen labia as Benjamin thrust his tongue into her mouth. She moaned, the deliciously decadent feeling of having them both pleasure her winding her climax ever closer.

And then, as if by some unknown signal, both men began to move faster, more forcefully. Samuel lifted her knees, opening her wider as he rubbed his hard cock against her pussy. He thrust into her just as Benjamin found her nipple and bit down. Her entire body was alight with arousal, heavy, aching, throbbing.

Samuel didn't give her time to adjust. He simply thrust into her again and again, his wide cock filling her, stretching her, claiming her. She ran a hand through Benjamin's hair, holding him to her, pressing him harder against her breast, asking for something she didn't really understand. Slippery fingers found her clit, squeezing and caressing the swollen bud as Benjamin used his fangs to pierce the soft flesh of her breast.

She screamed, arching her back, begging for more, as her arousal spun wildly out of control. Samuel bent over her, sucked the other breast into his mouth, and bit down.

Overwhelmed, orgasm exploded through her, brilliant swirling lights bursting in her mind as her body shook violently. Instinct took over, her body undulating against them, as she moaned, gasping, shivering, sobbing as heat fizzed in her blood and sensation took over. Every inch of her felt scorched, sated, finally, gloriously complete.

Eventually, both men gentled their assault, licking her breasts soothingly, dragging their sharp teeth over the sensitive flesh as liquid heat pulsed through every inch of her body.

Gasping for air, Skye held her men close, almost afraid to let go, terrified that she was only dreaming, but then Samuel moved away, and Benjamin rolled her over and lifted her to her hands and knees.

"Suck him, baby girl," he said as he eased his cock into her pussy. She opened her lips, tasting her own flavor as she licked Samuel's cock from root to tip before sucking the head into her mouth. Unlike the violence of moments ago, both men moved slowly, their soft groans and gentle movements somehow soothing her and inflaming her arousal at the same time.

Calloused hands stroked her everywhere, her ass and thighs tingling as Benjamin ran his fingers all over her flesh. Samuel caressed her face, his soft touch unable to hide the need coursing through him. She tightened the suction on his cock, moaning as he thrust a little harder, pushed a little deeper, groaned his need a little louder.

And then Benjamin started to move more quickly, thrusting harder and harder into her swollen pussy, the slippery flesh gripping him tighter as her own release drew closer. He groaned, ramming his cock into her again and again as Samuel did the same with her mouth.

And then heat exploded outward, every cell going into meltdown, her body shaking violently in release. She felt Benjamin join her, filling her with his seed. She cried out as Samuel pulled out of her mouth, but moaned in pleasure when he took Benjamin's place, flipped her onto her back, and then thrust hard and fast into her pussy.

He lifted her hips, kneading her ass cheeks, dragging her unresisting body against his again and again and again. And then he thrust to the hilt, jamming his cock inside her as his release began. His fingers found her clit, dancing furiously over the hypersensitive flesh, forcing her into mind-blowing orgasm once more.

When she finally came back down to earth, she sighed happily as both men slid onto the bed and pressed her between them. Exhausted, she snuggled closer, intending only to close her eyes for a moment.

* * * *

"She's asleep," Benjamin whispered to Samuel as he gazed at Skye's beautiful face. She wore a contented smile, her breathing relaxed, and her skin glowing from her recent orgasms. He wanted to lie here, just watching her sleep, but too soon duty called.

He dragged a blanket over Skye as he heard the soft knock on the connecting door. A moment later Thomas stepped into the room. Unfazed by Benjamin's nudity—werewolves didn't have the same hang-ups as humans when it came to being au naturel—Thomas reported their findings as Benjamin dragged his clothes back on.

"We've taken two vampires into custody. We're fairly certain that they are the ones who attacked Skye—I can still smell trace amounts of her blood on them—but we need to get a positive ID before we call in a pickup crew."

Benjamin glanced at the woman sleeping so peacefully in Samuel's arms and wondered if there was any other way to deal with this situation. Unfortunately, just like humans, they had rules and procedures to follow, and their bosses would be none too pleased if they sent in criminals for processing without ticking all the boxes first.

Samuel gave him a sad smile but nodded his agreement to their only real course of action.

"Okay, give us a few minutes to wake Skye and we'll join you. Where are you holding them?"

"Wilson managed to get them all the way into his motel room with the promise of fresh human." Thomas smiled gleefully. It wasn't usually so easy to acquire their targets. They must have been fairly young vampires if they didn't recognize a vampire from a PUP squad. Most older paranormals recognized them simply by the way they spoke and the confident way they moved. There was just something about working in the squads that gave the men and women a distinctive aura. Of course, with Benjamin's squad having worked together for over fifty years, it was probably even more obvious.

"Do we know who sired them?"

"Not yet, but I'm guessing they're only a year old at the most. One of them matches the description of a human doctor wanted for malpractice who went missing only a few months ago. The other has a 'homeless drug addict' sort of vibe."

Benjamin nodded. It wasn't unusual for homeless people to end up on the vampire food chain—who would believe them if they told the human authorities?—but it was very out of character to turn them. Most vampires were happy to keep their community small and inconspicuous and, until Skye, Benjamin had been one to agree with them.

"Okay, we'll meet you there in ten minutes."

Thomas nodded and left the room. If he knew how his friend's mind worked—and after fifty years working together, how could he not?—Thomas would not only know who the vampires were in their human lives but when, where, how, why they were transformed into vampires and who made them by the end of the night.

Samuel still held Skye close, his concern for her obvious in every stiff muscle. Physically they would protect her from any danger, but they had no defense against the mental anguish identifying her attackers might cause.

He briefly considered tracking down the nearest one-way mirror and putting her behind it, but it would be a considerable delay, and the longer they waited to catch the third vampire involved in the attack, the more chance they had that he would kill again.

Samuel was probably thinking the exact same things. It appeared that he came to the same conclusion when he sighed heavily and gently shook Skye awake.

"We're sorry, sweetheart, but we need your help."

* * * *

Her help?

The past couple of days, when she hadn't been sleeping, she'd been trying not to think about how useless she felt. She was usually the one helping other people out, not the damsel in distress, so it felt very weird to be dependent on these two men. Not that she wasn't enjoying their attentions. She sat up, grinning at the delicious soreness between her thighs. Simply pressing her legs together sent a rush of heat crashing over her.

But they needed her help. Help she was more than willing to give.

Samuel lifted her into his arms, carrying her to the bathroom as Benjamin smiled indulgently.

"We're sorry to do this to you, baby girl, but we think we've apprehended the two vampires who drained you. We need you to confirm that we got the right guys."

* * * *

Benjamin watched Skye closely. She looked a little nervous, but it was Samuel's arms tightening around her that got most of her attention. Her gaze bounced between the two of them as Samuel slowly lowered her to her feet.

"You'll be there?" she asked with a smile, obviously trying to hide her anxiety.

"Absolutely," Samuel said in a voice that sounded like he was chewing nails. "But you don't have to do this. We can find another way."

Seemingly confused by Samuel's statement, Skye sought Benjamin's gaze once more. He shrugged, wanting to protect her just as much as Samuel did, but aware enough of both the situation and the lady's stubborn streak to know the wisest choice was to leave the decision up to her. When she hesitated, Benjamin decided that it was probably best that she know all options and their consequences.

"A witness to the attack being able to identify them is the easiest way, but it does mean that they'll see you face-to-face. Thomas says he can smell trace amounts of your human blood on them, but with you no longer being human, the case would balance solely on

Thomas's testimony—a situation we try to avoid if at all possible. We might be trusted operatives, but that doesn't guarantee we'll always be believed." She shook her head, and he took that as her rejecting the second option. "Our third option is to find someone from the club that night who saw you leave with your attackers. The trouble with that is no one else seems to have witnessed the attack, so they'd only be testifying that you left the club with them. We have no laws against compelling humans, so we really only have the fact that they were in the general area when the attack took place—circumstantial evidence at best."

Samuel turned on the shower, adjusted the temperature, and dragged Skye under the warm water with him. He started washing her down, apparently trying to distract her, but the woman proved just how stubborn she was by holding his hands away and turning to face him.

"Why don't you want me to do this? What harm can come to me if I identify my attackers?"

Samuel smiled softly, but it was obvious by his expression that he was both proud and afraid for her in that moment.

"I just wish we had a proper interview room so that you wouldn't have to come face-to-face with the men who stole your human life. I want to protect you from that. You've been through enough already."

Skye reached up to touch his cheek, her concern for him obvious. "I'm not a delicate flower. In many ways I *need* to do this. I could never forgive myself if someone else got killed because I was too scared to do the right thing."

Samuel pulled her into a crushing embrace, the raw emotion almost too private for Benjamin to witness. "We will be right beside you," he said quietly. "We won't let them anywhere near you."

"I believe you," she said with a soft smile.

Chapter Five

Samuel held Skye's hand tightly in his own, unprepared for the fear that coursed through him. Dangerous situations had always thrilled him, gotten his adrenaline pumping, but when it was Skye's safety at risk, he was shaking like a leaf in a tornado. It was difficult to comprehend how important she'd become to him so quickly.

He heard the confident, cultured voice of the man he assumed was the missing doctor, but judging by his words, it was even clearer now that he knew nothing about the Ruling Body or the dictates all paranormals were required to live by. He was currently threatening legal action for false detention despite the fact that paranormals had no such system of compensation and had no need to answer to the human one.

"Skye," Benjamin said in a soothing tone. "Are these the men who attacked you?"

"Yes," she said, trying valiantly to hide the shudder that being so close to these men evoked. Samuel truly wished he'd been able to save her this trauma, but it was also interesting to see her strength of character. Her voice was clear, her eyes wide open, and her gaze holding theirs unflinchingly.

"Good enough for me," Alex said with a wink just for Skye. "Now we can get down to the fun part of the evening."

"F–Fun p–part?" the younger of the two men asked. Judging by the man's painfully thin frame, he was probably a drug addict before he'd been bitten. The transformation basically froze a person's build and physique at the point of change, so even if he was stronger than he looked, thanks to his vampire status, his outward appearance would never change from that of a gaunt, malnourished drug addict.

"Sure," Thomas said in his most friendly voice, "now that we know we've got the right vamps we can move on to the information gathering phase." He picked up a small letter opener that appeared to be made of silver.

Samuel almost laughed when he realized that his team had secured the two vampires to their chairs with silver chains. They were the delicate necklace type but it didn't take much silver to hold a new vamp down. It would require considerably more effort to restrain the older and more experienced vampires in their team, but it did however reinforce just how newly made these vampires really were.

He pulled Skye closer, wanting to leave, but sensing her need to be here as her attackers confessed all—well, hopefully, confessed all. It would be a damn sight easier if they just gave up their "friend's" details, but Samuel was beginning to suspect that the guy was also their sire. It was much harder for a vampire to betray his or her maker, and it most likely explained why these guys were so clueless. Despite their sire's instinct to keep them around, he'd never taught them anything they needed to know.

Samuel carefully hid his smile when he noticed that Thomas and Adam both wore rubber gloves as if the silver could hurt them. It was a little known fact that it was liquid mercury and not silver that could fatally harm werewolves—a fact werewolves were quite willing to go to extraordinary lengths to hide. Samuel couldn't blame them. He would have happily hidden the truth about a vampire's weaknesses, but these days it seemed nearly everybody who'd read a book, seen a movie, or watched a TV knew how to kill a vampire. Thankfully most thought their existence pure fiction.

Alex moved closer to the younger-looking fledgling vampire and held the letter opener as if he planned to cut into the man's face. The ex-drug addict looked terrified, proving that Alex had chosen the right target. The man they suspected had once been a human doctor just looked bored.

"Look, man," Thomas said in a faked sympathetic tone, "my partner here likes this part of the job. Me? Not so much, so maybe you can do me a favor and just tell us what we want to know before we get to the screaming part."

Samuel felt Skye tense up in his arms, but he squeezed her gently and tried to ease her concern with his touch. He'd seen Thomas and Alex do their good cop, bad cop routine so many times that he could practically predict how things would go from here on out.

"Wh–What d–do y–y–you want to know?"

"Where is the third vampire? The one who killed the red-haired woman?"

The older man smirked, but the younger shook his head in panic. "We don't know. When we woke up, he was just gone. We don't know where he went."

"Was he your sire?"

The younger man looked to the older for a moment before shrugging. Either he didn't know who his sire was or he didn't have a clue what the word meant. Samuel was leaning toward the latter.

"Do you know what name he was using?" Thomas had softened his tone, perhaps realizing that the young man in front of them had suffered considerably as a human child and had fared no better as a vampire.

"We just knew him as Ritchie. I don't know if that was his first name or family name." He glanced at his coaccused and seemed to shrink back from the man's anger.

The older man growled low in his throat, the sound more wolf than vampire. "You're as stupid as your whore of a mother," he said vehemently. "That's why Ritchie didn't fucking tell you anything. Fuck! I should have just let you die in that rat-infested alley."

* * * *

Benjamin ran a tired hand down his face. It took hours of patient, skilled interrogation but finally the story started to take shape. The older-looking vampire was indeed the missing doctor wanted for malpractice. Judging by additional information Wilson had been able to dig out of the closed police files, the man had been a cold-blooded killer long before he'd become a vampire. It was quite likely the reason "Ritchie" had turned him in the first place.

The younger-looking man fit the description of the doctor's biological son. It would seem that in a moment of uncharacteristic fatherly kindness the man had made his son into a vampire to save him from a drug overdose. Despite having been in his early twenties, the younger man seemed to have very little education and even less understanding of the world around him. He'd been shocked to learn that he didn't need to kill humans in order to feed.

"What will happen to them?" Skye asked as they finally stepped back into their own room.

Benjamin glanced at his watch. "A retrieval team will pick them up in a few hours and take them to headquarters for processing. Higgins—he's the administrative supervisor for PUP Squad Alpha— and a minimum of three Judiciaries will be assigned to the case so ultimately it's up to them. We're recommending that the doctor be terminated and his son given a chance at rehabilitation."

"Terminated? As in killed?"

Benjamin pulled her into his arms, holding her close as he tried to explain one of the harsher realities of paranormal life. "Yes, the human police files we were able to obtain say he's wanted for questioning in over fifteen suspicious deaths that happened while he was human. The attack on you proved that he's willing to continue killing as a vampire. We can't allow such an individual, with absolutely no conscience, to put the rest of the paranormal community in jeopardy."

She nodded against his chest, clearly disturbed by the death penalty that was part of paranormal life but, judging by her silence, also understanding the necessity of such a rule.

"So what happens now?"

"Now, baby girl, you get some rest."

"But I'm not tired," she said with a shy grin. "Maybe we can find something to work off all this excess energy."

"What? You mean like a board game or something?" he asked, deliberately misinterpreting her meaning.

She colored prettily in embarrassment. "I...um."

The woman was simply adorable when she was confused. Obviously, flirting wasn't something she'd done a lot of as a human, and when she dipped her head, he realized she'd misinterpreted his teasing. Feeling like a complete asshole, he lifted her chin and lowered his lips to hers. He kissed her softly, savoring the gentle contact, enjoying the soft whimper of need that escaped her control.

"Is this more like you had in mind?"

She nodded, her eyes closing as he took her lips again. He peeled her clothes off slowly, taking his time to enjoy each beautiful inch of flesh as it was revealed. By the time he had her completely naked, her knees wobbled so badly she'd likely have fallen on her ass if he let her go. Fortunately, he had no intention of letting her go.

He slid his hands all over her, learning her shape, tracing the hills and valleys of her breasts, lowering his head to flick his tongue over her nipples as heat rushed to his groin and his cock strained against the confines of his clothing. She moaned so deliciously as he ran his hands over her ass that he did it again and again, finally slapping the soft flesh as arousal gripped him tighter and he had to fight to stop himself from pushing her to the floor and taking her hard and fast.

She moaned again as he rubbed over the flesh he'd slapped, a ridiculous sense of ownership coursing through him as he traced the slightly raised welts where his fingers had landed. He needed to see them, needed to trace them with his tongue, needed to test if she enjoyed his rougher touch as much as it had seemed.

"Lean over the bed," he ordered even as he maneuvered her into the position he wanted. She went willingly, bending over and presenting her beautiful ass just the way he'd imagined. He'd smacked her rather hard, the outline of his hand quite clear on her pale skin. He leaned over to press soft kisses to the reddened flesh. "Did you enjoy this?"

He felt her tense up, felt her hesitate, but one whispered "yes" sent heated lightning streaking through his entire body. Unable to resist, he slapped the other cheek just as hard, watching as the skin turned colors right in front of him. She moaned, her pussy pulsing her need, the sweet smell of her arousal filling the room.

* * * *

Samuel entered the room slowly. He could hear the delicious whimpers that escaped his woman. For a brief moment he considered leaving Benjamin and Skye alone to get to know each other better, but the sight of her bent over the bed, her ass cheeks rosy red with Benjamin's handprint sent every dominant tendency he owned into overdrive.

Before he'd fully planned out what he wanted to do, Samuel had shucked his clothes and slid onto the bed in front of Skye. He helped her to stay in position, supporting her arms as he moved them off the mattress and onto his hips.

Needing to be certain that this was what Skye wanted, he tilted her face up and gazed into her eyes. They were half closed with her arousal, unfocused, unseeing for a moment before she finally gave him a lopsided smile. "Suck me, sweetheart," he said as he slid his hands into her hair and pressed his cock against her lips. She quickly opened her mouth, toying and teasing him with her tongue as his eyes damn near rolled into the back of his head. It was obvious she wasn't experienced, but her clumsy movements set him on fire in a way that the practiced attention of any other female would not.

She slowly lowered her mouth over him, taking him deep, caressing the underside with her tongue, before gradually lifting back up, suctioning her lips around him as she moved. As she reached the head of his cock, Benjamin spanked her ass, pushing her forward onto Samuel's erection once more. She did it again, the slow descent, the loving, warm caress, the hard suction as she moved back up. She moaned, the delicious vibration traveling the length of his cock as Benjamin slapped her again. She repeated the move, faster this time, taking him deeper, sucking him harder, moaning louder as Benjamin began to spank her over and over and over.

* * * *

Skye couldn't believe she was doing this. It was almost like watching someone else take over her body and do things she'd only ever imagined.

The skin on her ass burned, the heat pouring over her as her clit throbbed in time with her heartbeat. Each slap pushed her harder onto Samuel, his cock thrusting to the back of her throat as her own arousal dripped down her thighs. She felt his hands tighten in her hair, his moans growing more urgent, his cock swelling a moment before his flavor burst onto her tongue. She swallowed, surprised at the pleasant taste.

Yet she had but a moment to enjoy Samuel's orgasm before strong fingers dug into her hips and a hard cock probed her pussy lips. Benjamin rammed into her, not giving her time to adjust, claiming her, taking her, possessing her in the most elemental of ways. Samuel held her close, pushing her face against his neck as Benjamin fucked her harder and harder, violently thrusting into her needy, grasping pussy, her orgasm spiraling to unimagined heights as her mouth opened over Samuel's throat.

"Do it," he ordered, pressing her harder against his neck.

She tried to deny her need, tried to resist the nectar pulsing under the skin, tried to recall why she shouldn't do this, but then Benjamin grabbed her clit, his fingers dancing frantically over the swollen bud. "Do it," he ordered, pushing her face harder against Samuel, forcing her mouth open even as they pushed her body into orgasm.

She bit down, feeling the skin pop, feeling the blood flow, tasting Samuel's incredible flavor even as he grabbed her hand, wrapped it around his unexpectedly hard cock, and pumped it up and down. Warm cum splashed onto her breasts, the heat so shocking that she barely felt the slap against her thigh as Benjamin ordered her to come again.

Everything, *everything*, exploded into brilliant rainbow colors as her brain went into meltdown and her body shook with orgasm. Benjamin rode her hard, dragging her onto his cock, thrusting violently as he found his own release, groaning as he leaned over, pressed his lips to her neck, and bit down hard. She screamed, her entire being quaking as orgasm exploded through her once more.

"Fuck," Samuel said in a shocked tone as Benjamin gently pulled his fangs from her neck and licked at the wound. Still shaking, she did the same, carefully extracting her sharp teeth from Samuel's flesh, surprised to see the tiny holes close as she licked the skin clean.

"Holy shit," Benjamin said on a moan as he pulled his cock from her pussy, and helped her to practically fall into Samuel's lap. Samuel pulled her close and ran a hand through her hair over and over, his movements compulsive, his tension almost palpable.

"What is it?" she asked, her exhaustion quickly fleeing as she realized something was wrong.

"Shower time," Benjamin said as he lifted her from Samuel's arms and headed into the bathroom. She fought him, kicking her legs until he put her down.

"What is it?" she demanded of Samuel once more. Something was wrong. The pleasure of moments ago started to dilute, the shock of her wanton behavior, the guilt of letting two men take her so violently, the fear of being rejected, the weirdness of biting and being bitten and enjoying the hell out of it, wound through her brain.

Samuel must have finally gathered enough wits to realize she was upset because he stood, pulled her into his embrace, and ran his hand gently over her face. "It's nothing," he said in a reassuring voice. "I was just thanking our lucky stars our maker had more control than we do. If he'd felt even half the attraction to us the way we feel for you, I suspect we would have had to hand in our hetero membership cards a long time ago."

"I don't understand," she said, looking to Benjamin for an explanation. "What does that mean, exactly?"

A nasty suspicion was winding through her brain, and the insecure teenage girl she'd once been, the one who'd gotten rejected over and over for being too boring, was terrified that it might be true. When Benjamin seemed disinclined to explain, she took a deep fortifying breath and voiced her suspicion out loud. "Are you only attracted to me because you're the ones who changed me into a vampire?"

Samuel looked stricken by her question, but Benjamin shook his head slowly. "We don't know," he said quietly. "We don't know anything for sure."

"But you weren't attracted to me before you made me." It was an unfair accusation. They'd saved her life. They hadn't even known her before they'd made her a vampire. But rational thinking didn't seem to be part of the panic coursing through her heart. "Is that why I'm attracted to you? Is that why I let you…" Her voice broke, and the words trailed away. Shame at her wanton behavior drowned her in misery, her brain no longer working in tandem with her body. She was vaguely aware of Benjamin guiding her into the shower and washing her down, but the familiar excitement his touch had provoked was missing. "I want to go home," she said miserably. She knew she was overreacting. Hell, if her sister had been here, Jennifer would have told her to snap out of her selfish behavior and look at the problem from all angles, but all she could feel was the agony as pain tore through her heart.

* * * *

Samuel was still shaking. He had no answers for her. Neither he nor Benjamin had made any real connection to a female—human or otherwise—since they'd been turned into vampires. Sure, there'd been women in both their beds on and off over the decades, but none of them had evoked the feelings that Skye did. Whether that had something to do with him being one of her makers he had no idea.

"She's asleep," Benjamin said as he stepped into the room Alex and Thomas had been occupying. Despite cursing himself for the cowardly behavior, Samuel had run the moment Benjamin took Skye into the shower. He spent several minutes writing an updated report for their supervisor, carefully explaining who Skye was and how she'd survived the attack, and studiously ignoring his two squadmates in the room. In the fifty years they'd been working together, none of them had seen him this confused. Thankfully, Alex and Thomas had chosen this moment to take the unusual approach and mind their own business, not pushing at all for an explanation.

Samuel encrypted his e-mail, pressed send, and turned to his best friend. "She needs her sister," he said in a rough voice. Skye called Jennifer each evening as soon as she woke at sundown. Some days their conversation was brief, at other times much longer, but it was obvious to anyone within hearing distance that the two women were very close.

"I agree," Benjamin said, managing to surprise him. They were both very big believers in keeping information about paranormals out of human hands, but it would seem that Skye's need for her family overrode the concerns both of them held. "But we need to track down this 'Ritchie' guy before he kills again. We need to, all three of us, hold it together until we can complete this mission." He smiled encouragingly. "I'll do the paperwork to get some time off as soon as we get this done."

Samuel looked at his best friend, really looked at him for the first time in decades, and saw again that core of strength that had been the reason he'd followed the man into battle—both as human and as a vampire. "I'm sorry I fucked this up for you."

Benjamin looked shocked at his quiet words, shook his head as if to disagree, but then grinned and slapped him on the shoulder instead. "Let's just get the mission done. Then we'll figure out how to convince our reluctant woman that no matter where the attraction first came from she still belongs with us."

* * * *

Skye downloaded yet another book to her e-reader, staunchly ignoring the erotic romances. Well, technically she was trying to avoid all romance stories, but it was amazing how many mainstream books carried a romantic thread. Hell, even the murder mystery she'd just finished had ended with a happily ever after for the main characters. Sheesh, did the whole world revolve around love?

She glanced at Samuel working intently on his laptop. To describe the past several days as tense would be a serious understatement. Both Samuel and Benjamin had given her the space she'd insisted they all needed. She wasn't a slave to her hormones. She refused to mistake chemically induced lust for the love connection she'd always craved.

"Why do our hearts beat?" She asked the question out of curiosity, but more than wanting an answer she wanted to see the uncertainty wiped from Samuel's face. Alex had told her Samuel's nickname had been "The Iceman," but since meeting her he'd been anything but cold.

"I'm not really sure I know the answer," he said quietly. "I was once told that vampires are simply a different species to human. The blood that you drink from your maker starts the change on a genetic level, altering your cells and rewriting your DNA."

"So we're not 'the living dead'?"

"Far from it," he said with a soft smile. "We're very long lived, but we're not immortal. Eventually, we'll succumb to the ravages of age, albeit hundreds of years after our human bodies would have died."

"So the other stuff—casting no reflection in a mirror, needing permission to enter someone's home, a wooden stake to the heart, bursting into flames, holy water—that's all just made up?"

He laughed softly. "Humans have added to the legends over the years. I've never seen a vampire burst into flames in the sunshine, but our reaction to the sun's rays is rather immediate and quite horrible. The burns are very painful." He shrugged as if getting burned was not that big a deal. "I think the mirror thing was a way of blaming vampires for unexplained illnesses. Even if they couldn't see us, we must have been there stealing their energy." He grinned. "And I suspect the permission thing was one clever vampire's way of convincing humans that they were safe as long as they didn't invite a vampire in."

"I suppose that makes sense," she said as she tried to imagine life before widespread medical knowledge and small towns full of hysterical, superstitious folks trying to protect their families.

"A stake to heart, though, that's real. Our bodies can heal very quickly so we do have a chance if the stake is removed immediately, but any damage to the heart can be fatal. Just like any other living creature."

"So a bullet can kill us?"

"Depends on the bullet and where it hits. A low caliber hurts like hell, but our healing abilities quickly force the slug out and seal the wound."

"You know this firsthand?" she blurted in shock. Even though they'd explained what it was that PUP Squad Alpha did, she hadn't really associated their work with such mortal dangers.

"Yes, I've been shot," he said with another of those soft smiles, "but I've been lucky that both times the damage was minimal. Some of today's modern weapons are much more dangerous. There aren't many living creatures—human, paranormal, or otherwise—that could survive explosive rounds and rocket launchers."

"So you could..." She had to swallow the sudden lump in her throat before she could continue. "You could die in the line of duty? Just like a human soldier?"

He shrugged. "Our squad has been working together for nearly five decades. We're very good at what we do."

"I...but you could die." It probably sounded so lame, but somehow she'd convinced herself that Benjamin and Samuel and the rest of the squad were invincible. "What about—" She cut off her words as the main door of their motel room opened.

"Skye?" her sister asked in a small voice as she stepped into the room. "Are you all right?"

She practically flew across the room and grabbed her sister in a tight hug. It had only been ten days, but so many things had happened that it felt very much longer. "God, I missed you."

"Back at you, kid," Jennifer said in a husky voice. "Benjamin explained what happened. He also suggested I make sure you've fed before I let you hug me."

The reminder of what she was and what she was capable of had her thrusting her sister away from her. She took a step back, relieved at least to realize that she hadn't even considered biting Jennifer despite having had her face pressed against the vein throbbing at the side of her sister's throat. But just to be on the safe side Skye took another step back.

"Wait...he told you?"

"Yeah, well, I took a bit of convincing, but you know, you're my sister, and well, we're the only family we have left. If you're going to be a vampire, then the least I can do is support you."

Skye glanced at the wry expression on Benjamin's face before turning her attention back to her sister. "He wasn't lying. I am a vampire now."

Her sister smiled and nodded as if she were dealing with a particularly delusional individual. "I believe you," she said in a tone of voice that was far from genuine.

"She's proven to be a tough cookie to convince," Benjamin said with a laugh in his voice. "I even showed her my fangs, and she still thinks we're overgrown teenagers playing a fantasy game."

"But what about the undercover stuff? The whole 'keep the secret from humans' thing?" Skye asked.

"Occasionally, we make an exception," Benjamin said with a shrug.

"You did that for me?"

"Of course," Benjamin said, glancing at Samuel as he spoke. "We were going to wait until the mission was completed, but since the trail has taken us almost back to your hometown, we figured now was as good a time as any."

"We? You both did this?"

"Technically we all agreed. If Jennifer decided to break our confidence, it would put the whole squad in danger."

"The squad?" Jennifer asked with genuine confusion. "Don't you call a group of vampires a coven?"

"We do," Benjamin said with a laugh, "but in this particular case we do mean squad."

Jennifer looked to Skye. She wore her "what the hell?" face. "They're part of a Paranormal Undercover Protection squad," Skye volunteered. "Kind of like a Navy SEAL team but with fangs and claws."

"Claws?" Jennifer asked with a raised eyebrow.

"Yeah," she said, glancing at Benjamin to check if she was spilling some beans she wasn't supposed to. He nodded for her to continue. "Some of them are werewolves. Some of them are...other paranormals."

"Oh," her sister said, obviously trying very hard to appear diplomatic.

"It's okay if you don't believe us just yet, but we do ask that you keep the information to yourself," Benjamin said quietly.

"Of course," she said in a tone of voice that suggested she was starting to think she might be the crazy one. She jumped nearly half a foot into the air when Thomas opened the connecting door between the rooms.

Thomas sniffed the air, his gaze landing on Jennifer. A wide smile graced his face before he seemed to shake himself and get back to the matter at hand. "We just got a call from the owner of the club where Skye was attacked. He says he's got three unknown vampires on the premises. One of them fits the description Skye gave us. West, Adam, and Alex are on their way there now, but if this is our guy, they could use some vampire backup."

Samuel looked concerned, but he didn't object when Benjamin ordered Thomas to stay with Skye and Jennifer. After a brief kiss Benjamin left the room at preternatural speed. Samuel seemed to hesitate just a moment before he, too, kissed her and left the motel.

"Wh–What just happened?" Jennifer asked as her knees wobbled and she dropped into the chair behind her. "How did they disappear? I mean, they...they were standing there and...and now..."

Skye moved to her sister's side, grabbed her hand, and held on tight. "Breathe, sis," she said in what she hoped was a reassuring voice. "You'll get used to it."

Jennifer's half laugh, half guffaw suggested that it might be a long time coming. She turned her attention to Thomas, looked him up and down, and asked in a tone more rude than Skye had ever heard her sister use, "So what are you?"

Thomas gave her that charming smile Skye had come to associate with the man, lifted Jennifer's free hand to his mouth, and kissed the back of it in a gallant flourish that somehow seemed perfectly natural and not the corny move it could have been. "I'm a werewolf, but my friends call me Thomas."

"Uh-huh," Jennifer said skeptically, "and when am I going to see you turn into a wolf? Do I need to wait for a full moon?"

"Nope, I can show you right now, if you'd like."

Jennifer's eyes widened as Thomas started to undo his shirt. Whether her reaction was out of fear or curiosity Skye wasn't sure, but it was probably time to put a stop to Thomas's teasing. He was considered the ladies' man of the squad, and the last thing Jennifer needed right now was a playboy wolf hitting on her.

"Maybe later," Skye said, taking the seat beside her sister.

Thomas groaned in obvious disappointment, but he did refasten the buttons. "How abou—" He cut off his words, his relaxed demeanor morphing straight into full alert. "Call your makers."

"What? I don't have their cell numbers."

Thomas looked like he wanted to roll his eyes, but he turned his back on them, placing himself squarely between the two women and the front door. "Call them with your mind," he ordered in an agitated voice. "Shit, *do* it. Do it now!"

Taken aback by Thomas's barely leashed aggression, Skye mentally called to Benjamin and Samuel. She had no idea if she was doing it right, but she practically screamed their names in her mind. Fear pounded through her even harder when a soft knock sounded on the motel room door. Skye grabbed her sister, holding her behind Thomas, ready to do whatever it might take to protect her family.

"Stay here," Thomas ordered over his shoulder as he stepped toward the door.

Skye nodded, not willing to put her sister at risk for any reason.

But as Thomas got closer to the door, the tension drained from his shoulders. He turned to give them a reassuring smile. "It's my boss," he said. "Benjamin thought Higgins might drop by once he learned Benjamin and Samuel made a vampire on company time." He winked, letting them know it wasn't really that big a deal, and then turned back to the door. He unlocked the dead bolt and twisted the handle.

The door seemed to open too slowly, the fear in Skye's mind growing worse even despite Thomas's reassurance. The empty doorway just made her more jumpy, the horror-movie atmosphere growing more creepy. But then he was there, the vampire who'd killed an innocent woman, standing right in front of her. He'd moved faster than even Skye's new vampire-enhanced vision could follow. Thomas stepped forward, obviously confused by the man's behavior but still willing to risk his own life to protect them.

"Oh, such a brave puppy," the vampire said. He lunged at Thomas, aiming for the man's throat, but Thomas dropped to all fours, changing to a wolf as the sound of tearing fabric filled the room. The wolf also went for the throat, his sharp teeth gnashing at the intruder's shoulders as he caught Thomas around the middle, squeezing his ribcage tightly. The wolf clawed and bit, trying to free itself, but yelped in distress as the sound of cracking bones reached Skye's ears.

"Sorry, Tommy," the vampire said as he dropped the severely injured wolf to the ground, "but you always were one for being in the wrong place at the wrong time." He laughed and then kicked the wolf hard in the gut. "Now watch while I show you what happens when you can't tell friend from foe." He smiled maliciously as the wolf whined in pain. "Don't worry, puppy, I'll finish you off once I've dealt with these two. It's just that I've always found torture far more fun when I have someone to watch." He turned his attention to Skye for a moment before his gaze slid to Jennifer. "Well, would you look at that. Another pretty redhead for me to tear apart. How kind of you to bring her right to me. Come here, lovely."

Chapter Six

"Something's wrong," Samuel said as soon as they stepped into the crowded club.

Benjamin nodded in agreement. Something was definitely off. Alex spotted them, pushed his way through the crowd, and stopped close enough to give his situation report. "The club's empty of vampires. Not even the owner or any members of his coven are in the building. Adam is tracking a scent trail of blood, but it's turning us in circles. It feels like a deliberate setup."

"But why? For what purpose? The club owner surely knows not to—" Samuel's words cut off at the same moment Benjamin heard Skye's voice in his head.

"Skye," he managed to say as he ignored all protocols and used his preternatural speed to leave the club. It felt like the trip back to the motel took twice as long as it should have, Skye's terrified telepathic voice in his head spurring him to faster speeds.

Sense kicked in a moment before he burst into the motel room. Samuel did the same, a look of incredulity gracing his face as they both realized who was in the room.

"Come here, lovely," their supervisor said to one of the women inside.

* * * *

Jennifer began to move toward him, her outward calm eerily familiar. Skye held her tight, stopping her forward movement, but it took way more effort than it should have to stop a human. Apparently being compelled by a vampire also gave the victim an inhuman strength.

"Why are you doing this?" Skye asked, hoping only to stall the man long enough for Samuel and Benjamin to get back to the motel.

"Because you have caused me way more aggravation than you should have. If those idiots had just drained you properly, there wouldn't have been enough of you left to save, and I wouldn't have had to go cleaning up their mess."

"I don't understand," Skye said, playing her dumb-blonde card for all it was worth. "What mess?" Blonde jokes had been the bane of her existence her entire life—it was even why Jennifer dyed her hair red—but maybe this time Skye could make the common assumption that hair color somehow affected her intelligence work for her. "You know, like, I'm just, you know, confused is all. I mean, why are you such a meanie?"

She almost gagged on the out-of-character words, but judging by the guy's derogatory laugh he was buying the act. Skye somehow sensed Benjamin and Samuel were close. She wasn't sure if the other vampire could sense them also, so she tried to keep his focus elsewhere while her men came up with a rescue plan. At least that's what she hoped they were doing.

"Why redheads? Is that, like, you know, your favorite color or something?"

Jennifer had stopped trying to walk out of her embrace, so Skye hoped that meant she was distracting the guy enough to disrupt his ability to compel humans. But then the vampire turned sharply toward the door, obviously sensing Skye's makers on the other side. He lunged for her, but she was ready for it, ducking out of the way, practically throwing her sister across the room as the front door and the bathroom door opened simultaneously. Two loud gunshots reverberated through the room, but it was the explosion of the bullets on impact that tore a gaping hole in the vampire's chest.

Skye pushed her sister into the corner, covering Jennifer with her own body as blood and guts flew through the air and covered almost everything in the room.

They were both shaking violently when Samuel touched her lightly on the back a few moments later. "Are you okay?" Skye wanted to throw herself into his arms, but Jennifer was shuddering in reaction, tears streaming down her face, her understanding of the world around her obviously turned on its head, and Skye didn't want to leave her.

"We're fine," Skye said, trying to convey how glad she was that they'd arrived when they did. "Is Thomas still alive?"

"Thomas!" Jennifer said as she tried to scramble out of Skye's embrace. Skye went with her, fear for the werewolf who'd risked his life to save theirs overriding all other concerns. She did manage to at least shield Jennifer from the gory sight of the dead vampire though.

"He's going to be fine," Adam said with a small smile as they crouched down near the wolf's head. "Looks like the bastard broke every bone in Thomas's ribcage, but nothing that can't heal on its own. He'll hurt for a while, but he'll be good as new in a couple hours."

"Really?" Jennifer asked in a soft voice. She leaned over and gently stroked the wolf's muzzle. Skye's sister had always had a kind heart, but it was unusual for her to get so close to a dog of any kind. Having been bitten as a child, Jennifer's avoidance of man's best friend was almost legendary. Of course, none of the furry critters they'd met before now had been werewolves or had been a man who'd saved their lives.

Surprisingly, Adam put his arm around Jennifer, holding her close as she sat caressing the wolf's fur. Skye was a little taken aback to see her sister lean her head on Adam's chest. They hadn't even actually met, but he held her closer, and Skye realized that, for the moment at least, her sister was in good hands. She squeezed Jennifer's fingers slightly and then let go so that she could move to where Samuel and Benjamin were standing with the rest of the team.

Benjamin saw her approach, and when she stopped a few feet away, uncertain of her welcome, he leaned over and dragged her into the space between him and Samuel. Benjamin kept his arm around her shoulder, but he pressed her against Samuel's side at the same time. Samuel put his arm around her middle, his hesitation only momentary before he held on tight.

"Skye, is this the vampire who killed the woman the night you were attacked?" Wilson sounded so formal, and for a moment she worried what that meant.

"Yes," she said with a brief glance at the corpse lying in the middle of the room with a massive hole in its chest. She stiffened as images of that horrific first night replayed in her head. There was absolutely no doubt in her mind that they had the right vampire.

"Good," Wilson said with a kind smile. "That will make it far easier to explain to the Judiciaries why we just killed our boss."

"Although," Alex said with a tight smile, "the fact that he lied about his age, and tried to kill a PUP squad member should be plenty of explanation even without eyewitness testimony."

"His age?" Skye asked, trying to figure out what his age had to do with anything.

"That," Benjamin said, pointing a thumb over his shoulder but not turning around, "is not the corpse of a seven-hundred-year-old vampire."

"How can you tell?" Call it morbid curiosity, but she really wanted to know.

"When a vampire dies the body tends to decay very rapidly. The older we are the faster it happens. At seven hundred years of age the corpse and all of its bodily fluids should have decayed to dust practically before it hit the ground. As you can see by the mess, that didn't happen. He was probably closer to seventy or eighty years old, give or take a few years."

"So he wasn't who he said he was?"

"No, baby girl, he wasn't," Benjamin said as he pressed a kiss to her forehead. But then another thought occurred to her and she looked around the room frantically.

"What about the noise? Shouldn't we be preparing a story for the police? Surely someone heard the bullets."

"Relax, sweetheart, we used silencers. The sound would only have seemed loud because of your vampire hearing. We'll call a pixie cleanup crew to take care of the mess."

"Pixie?" she asked in a small, squeaky voice.

Samuel must have heard how overwhelmed she was feeling just by the tone of her voice. "We'll leave the explanation of that for another day."

"Let's get the paperwork done," Benjamin said as he squeezed her gently and then turned to check on Thomas. "I think we should all plan on taking some time off. Samuel and I have been considering a long holiday anyway, but with the mission turning out the way it has, we're probably all liable to be stood down from active duty while the Judiciaries review the mission briefs."

"True," Adam said with a happy smile. "It's probably about time I took Thomas home to his mama. That mean old lady's liable to rip me a new one if I don't get him home for Thanksgiving this year." The wolf that was Thomas growled low in its throat, but by Adam's happy smile it seemed that it was probably a long-running joke. "And besides, I'd rather be on leave than have to face a desk job while the Judiciaries take their sweet time dottin' eyes and crossin' tees."

The others all murmured in agreement.

* * * *

Skye woke to her sister's smiling face.

"Wow, when that sun comes up you really go down for the count. They weren't kidding."

Skye glanced around her and finally realized that she was in her sister's guest room. "So you believe me now?" she asked unsteadily.

Jennifer smiled and shrugged. "Seeing a man morph into a wolf in front of my eyes kind of squashed my skepticism."

"Is Thomas okay?" Skye asked. She remembered Adam's reassurance from earlier, but a lot could have changed in the eight hours that she'd slept like the dead.

"He's going to be fine. Adam called a few hours ago to let Benjamin know they'd arrived home safe and sound."

"Where's home?" Skye asked. There was just something about the way her sister's smile softened and her eyes glistened when she spoke about the two wolves that made Skye wonder if she'd missed much more than just their departure.

"Their families live in a gated community at the top of some mountain about an eight-hour drive from here," Jennifer said quickly, as if it were no big deal.

"You like them," Skye said with a smile on her lips.

Jennifer gave her a lopsided grin, but then released a breathy laugh and shook her head. "What's not to like? They're gallant, protective, arrogant, good-looking sweethearts who are way out of my league." Skye opened her mouth to correct her. Jennifer was an amazing woman who deserved to be happy, but she held up a hand to stop Skye's words. "And they are werewolves who live a long way from here and spend most of their time traveling around the country on one mission or another."

Skye smiled sadly. Her sister had a point. Even if she could accept and overcome the paranormal aspect, there was still the fact that she'd barely see them anyway. A fact that suddenly hammered home to Skye the possibly bleak future she herself faced. It didn't matter where the initial attraction had come from. She was irrevocably in love with both her men, but without a shadow of a doubt Benjamin and Samuel's lives were far easier without her hanging around.

"Where are they?" she asked her sister with a heavy heart. Maybe they'd already left. They'd taught her what she needed to know to be a good little vampire. Her hometown had more than a few of her kind so she wouldn't be without assistance if she needed it, and the mission was complete so she was no longer in danger. Despite what they'd said about taking time off, it was quite possible they'd gone onto their next mission without a backward glance.

"They're at the motel making sure that the pixies did their jobs properly."

"Oh," Skye said, feeling a little less downhearted just knowing that they were still in the area.

"They had hoped to be back before you woke up."

"They did?"

"Of course they did," Jennifer said with a strange smile on her face. "I got the impression that they were both in love with you. Why wouldn't they be here? Don't you like them?"

"Of course I like them. Hell, I'm in love with them, but..." She had to swallow that stupid lump of fear crowding her throat before she could force out the rest of the words. "But, they...they're only attracted to me because they made me a vampire."

"So what does that mean? Do they have other women? What about the vampires who made them? Holy hell, does that mean that every vampire they make is going to fall in love with them? Shit, no wonder vampires have an image that includes orgies and sexual deviancy."

"Don't believe everything you read," Benjamin said as he and Samuel walked into the bedroom. Skye had been so focused on her own fears that she hadn't even sensed them coming into the house, but she was very grateful to see her men. She just hoped that they weren't coming to say good-bye. "The very fact that our own maker was able to resist us proves that the base attraction connected with the change can be denied. We only know of a handful of new fledglings, but only one of them, as far as we know, has a romantic relationship with her maker."

"Oh," Skye said, cringing at the nonword that was coming out of her mouth far too often lately.

"Baby girl," Benjamin said, "please don't leave us. We know it's not going to be easy to build a relationship with all three of us, but can you please just give things a chance?"

"What do I do when you guys are working? I mean, don't you travel all over the country?" Why was she arguing? This was what she wanted, wasn't it? But then her sister's words from moments ago lodged in her brain, and she had a hard time shoving them aside. How could they keep a relationship going if the men were always on a mission? Was it better to try and hold on to what might be or to make a clean break now before everyone got hurt? And, hell, was this even her thinking it? Moments ago she'd been ready to beg them to keep her.

Confused as hell by her own inner workings, she almost didn't see the devastation of Samuel's face. "It's okay, sweetheart," he said as he placed a calloused hand against her cheek. "Whatever you want to decide here will be fine. We just want you to be happy."

"But I am," she blurted out. "I mean I was...I will be...I want to try. I want to hold on to both of you." She blinked away the tears filming her eyes as Samuel crushed her in his embrace.

"We want that, too," he said in a voice tight with emotion.

She felt Benjamin's hand touch the back of her head, the gesture very loving. "We've organized to take the next six months off active duty. We'll find a compromise that works for all of us after that."

"Okay," Skye said as tears of joy and relief ran down her face. "I'd like that very much."

"And I think that's my cue to leave," Jennifer said in a teasing tone. "I have...er...errands to run, people to see, things to buy. I mean I could be at least, I don't know, two, three hours maybe."

"Thanks, Jen," Skye said gratefully. "You are an amazing sister."

"Back at you, kid," she said with a wink before leaving the room. A few moments later Skye heard her sister leave the house, pulling the front door closed tightly.

"Hmmm," Benjamin said as he slid onto the other side of the bed. "Two, maybe three hours, whatever shall we do with the time?"

Skye giggled at his teasing tone, but moaned at the firm hands that caressed her all over. "M–Maybe we can read a b–book," she said unsteadily.

"Only if," Samuel said in between placing soft kisses on her shoulders as he peeled her shirt away, "it's one of those ménage romance novels you were reading back at the motel."

Embarrassment heated her blood. "You knew about that?"

It was Samuel's turn at awkwardness. He stopped kissing her, seeming to weigh his words before he tried to explain. "It's a standard mission protocol to monitor the upload and download streams in the same Wi-Fi and cell phone area. Wilson mentioned that someone was downloading sexy books." She must have looked horrified by that news because Samuel started talking more quickly. "He had no idea who it was. It could have been anyone staying in that motel. He just mentioned it in passing, and we sort of figured it out because of the way you reacted to the books you were reading."

She wasn't sure that made it any better, but then Benjamin pushed the covers away, hooked his fingers into her pajama bottoms, and dragged them to her ankles. Thoroughly distracted, Skye moaned when he pressed hot, wet kisses against her flesh, pushing her legs wider as he managed to untangle the material from her feet.

The first touch of his tongue on her pussy was like coming home. Simply put, this was where she belonged, between her men. Samuel took her mouth, kissing her aggressively as Benjamin lapped at her folds in lazy counterpoint. Her entire body tingled as they each managed to ignite her arousal. Moaning softly, Skye dragged at Samuel's clothes as Benjamin slid his hands under her thighs and lifted her pussy to his mouth. He started thrusting his stiffened tongue into her channel, fucking her hard and fast as she writhed against his hold.

"Please," she said on a whimper, not really sure what she was begging for, but certain she'd go mad if they didn't provide it.

"Do you trust us?" Samuel asked as Benjamin lifted his head and thrust his fingers deep into her pussy. They both watched her closely, waiting for her answer. She nodded frantically, willing to follow them to the ends of the earth if they'd just not stop what they were doing right now.

Benjamin's fingers slid into her pussy over and over, her juices coating her thighs and running down the crack of her ass. His fingers followed, toying with the puckered muscle of her anus. She moved away, fear overriding her reassurance from just moments ago.

"Have you ever had a man in your ass?" Samuel asked as he seemed to watch the play of emotions over her face.

Breathlessly she tried to explain her reaction. "O–Only once. It hurt like hell, even several days later."

Both men stopped moving. Their hands touched her, but they didn't caress, didn't arouse, didn't enflame. She whimpered as she imagined their emotional withdrawal. "Please," she begged. Holy hell, could she be any more pathetic?

"Shhh," Benjamin said as he leaned over and kissed her, the taste of her own juices still on his lips. "You're a vampire now, so you are much stronger than you realize. You also have two men who plan to take their time preparing you." She nodded enthusiastically, so relieved that they weren't about to leave the room that she almost missed the finger that probed her anus. Benjamin's touch was gentle, soothing, not at all what she remembered of her one and only foray into anal play.

* * * *

Benjamin watched her closely, careful to move his finger slowly, making certain that she was enjoying his touch, not simply tolerating it. He and Samuel needed their woman to enjoy what they had planned, not stoically endure because she thought it was what they wanted.

But then Skye let out a little moan, coloring in embarrassment as she pushed against his finger in wanton need. That's what he'd been waiting for. Samuel handed him the lube they'd bought earlier and went back to kissing Skye, caressing her breasts, tweaking her nipples, keeping her arousal high, as Benjamin pushed a second finger into her ass. He scissored them, gently loosening her anal muscles, watching closely for signs of discomfort.

When he added a third, her muscles pulsed around his fingers, caressing the invading digits, squeezing him harder as her orgasm approached. He leaned over her, capturing her clit with his lips, using them to nibble and caress the taut bud. She cried out, lifting her hips and then pushing down onto his fingers, over and over again, her need obvious, her movements frantic. He sucked on her clit, flicking the swollen flesh with his tongue, tormenting her until she exploded into orgasm.

Benjamin moved back, dragging at his clothes, desperate to be inside her. She was still screaming her climax when he lifted her hips and thrust his cock straight into her pussy. He rode her orgasm, loving the feel of her pussy walls grasping and releasing his erection. Over and over he thrust into her, groaning his own delight as he nearly lost himself in her sweetness.

Eventually they gentled her with long sweeping strokes and soft kisses as she caught her breath and finally stopped shaking all over.

Exhausted, she let Benjamin move her pliant body to the position he wanted, and she didn't flinch at all when he pushed his fingers back into her ass. He lifted her legs higher, tucking her knees close to her chest, as he lined his cock up with her back passage and slowly breached the tight ring of muscle.

She moaned, trying to lift onto him, but he controlled her, stopping her movement, wanting to make this experience perfect for her. He ground his teeth together, controlling his own need to take her forcefully. In and out slowly, the gentle rhythm not nearly enough to satisfy them, but the absence of pain very important to all three.

Samuel rolled off the bed, stripping his clothes away as he nodded to Benjamin. He eased out of Skye's ass as Samuel lay down on the bed beside them.

"Ride him, baby girl," Benjamin said as he helped Skye lower onto Samuel's cock. All three of them moaned as she took him deep and leaned forward to press her lips against his mouth. Samuel had his legs hanging over the edge of the bed, his hands wrapped around Skye's knees so that she wouldn't slide off. That left room enough for Benjamin to step between their legs, his cock pulsing pre-cum as his best friend and his woman fucked each other. He caressed her ass, happy to just watch for the moment, but then Samuel slid his hands higher, opening her ass cheeks, and the temptation to join in was suddenly irresistible. Samuel held her still, pressing her down against him as Benjamin pressed his cock against her ass and prepared to slide home.

* * * *

Skye was on the edge of a precipice, so turned on that even being held down wasn't helping to cool her arousal. But then Benjamin pushed his cock against her ass, and suddenly she needed to be joined to both of them more than she needed orgasm.

He moved slowly, easing in and backing away in short, slow thrusts, giving her body time to adjust, before moving a little deeper, pushing a little harder, thrusting a little faster.

She moaned at the delicious sensations swirling through her, gasping as unexpected orgasm pulsed through her. But it was the reaction from her men that tipped everything into overdrive.

Groaning their pleasure, Benjamin and Samuel lifted her between them, thrusting in counterpoint, one slamming in as the other pulled out. They hadn't been kidding about the vampire part. Not only didn't it hurt, but it also sent her into the most heart-pounding, soul-stirring, breath-stealing orgasm she'd never imagined.

Screaming, unable to stop herself, she worked with them, slamming down onto Samuel's cock, lifting up onto Benjamin's. Both men groaned, their cocks seeming to grow a moment before they pulsed deep in her body, both pushing to the hilt, holding her close, caressing her lovingly.

Her own climax swelled, bursting over her one more time in a flood of liquid heat.

Pinned between her men, all three of them panting for air, Skye knew without a shadow of a doubt that this was where she belonged. It didn't matter where the attraction had first come from, it only mattered what they did with it.

"I love you. I love you both," she said breathlessly, grateful for vampire hearing that would have helped her soft words make it to their ears.

"Thank fuck for that," Benjamin said with a laugh. "We were quite prepared to keep you prisoner in this bedroom until you realized just how much we both love and need you. Be ours, Skye. Stay with us always."

She nodded, tears gathering in her eyes as she kissed Benjamin over her shoulder. The angle was awkward, the connection difficult, but with Samuel kissing the other side of her face, the sloppy kiss was somehow perfect.

"We love you, sweetheart," Samuel said against her ear, "and we're never letting you go."

"You're stuck with us, baby girl," Benjamin said with a laugh.

And she couldn't think of any place she'd rather be stuck.

Epilogue

Benjamin watched Skye and Samuel play in the snow, stifling a laugh when a large snowball hit Skye in the stomach, smashing to pieces and flinging the soft ice in every possible direction. She screeched with laugher, dodged the second ball Samuel lobbed her way, and returned the favor, catching Samuel high on his forehead. He smiled, growled, and then made a show of chasing her at preternatural speed around the huge snowman they'd just finished building.

Skye had thought them crazy when they'd suggested a holiday at a ski lodge in the middle of nowhere. Fortunately, when they'd explained that the lodge was owned by bear-shifters and for six weeks a year they restricted bookings to only paranormal visitors, she'd been more than happy to let go of the very human idea of a beach holiday. While a moonlit beach stroll did sound appealing, it was the short nights and long days that made the trip impractical. This high in the mountains, this time of year, they could literally go days without seeing the sun. A much better environment for vampires.

Dyson and Thomas appearing in front of him was annoying as hell.

Dyson grinned, patting Thomas on the shoulder when the wolf looked green enough to throw up. Despite the fact that every member of his squad was prepared to use slip travel in an emergency, it was not a favored transport for any of them—well, except for Dyson, Angus, and Alex, who'd been born to it. Everyone else ended up feeling nauseous, werewolves and vampires included.

"What do you want?" Samuel asked in a grumpy-sounding voice. They'd been on vacation for less than three months.

The investigation into the case had been closed a few weeks ago even though they hadn't been able to trace the e-mail that had originally tipped them off. Considering that the unknown sender potentially saved dozens of lives, the Judiciaries had decided to leave well enough alone—for now. The club owner had also been found innocent of making a false report. He hadn't even been at his bar that night, so he was unlikely to be the one who made the call. They were still piecing together who their former boss had actually been. The current theory was that he took on the identity of his maker after the vampire had died and that was how "Ritchie" had been able to work his way into such a high position in the PUP teams. Who he'd been before becoming a vampire was still unknown.

Samuel, Benjamin, and the rest of PUP Squad Alpha had already been cleared of any wrongdoing and were approved for active duty once more. But it was because of the woman heading over to them that they'd decided to take the full six months' leave. Sure, they'd ironed out most of their issues in the first month or two, but just spending time together uninterrupted had been what Benjamin, Skye, and Samuel had been enjoying the most.

"Sorry, Skye," Thomas said as he greeted her with a brief hug, "but we have a situation developing, and we could really use your husbands' help."

"Sure," she said with a bright smile to hide the worry he knew she was feeling. "I'll just go grab something to drink."

Benjamin wanted her to stay, wanted to call her back so he could hold her in his arms, but he also wanted to hear what his squadmates had to say before upsetting Skye needlessly. It was obvious by Thomas and Dyson's demeanor that they had a serious problem on their hands.

Samuel arched an eyebrow as he moved closer and then waited for Thomas to explain.

"Human police have reports of three murders in the past two days. All of them are victims of pixie assassins. The victims have all been human, Ben." He shook his head as if he still couldn't quite believe the information himself.

"They've always restricted their activities to paranormal beings. Why would they suddenly go after humans? It doesn't make any sense. Do we know who hired them?" Pixies never worked for free, so it was very likely someone else was paying for the assassinations.

"We're not sure," Dyson said, looking very uncomfortable. "None of the human victims had any paranormal contact. They didn't know each other. All three were from different socioeconomic backgrounds. The only thing they had in common was their age, twenty-seven, and their gender, female, otherwise the attacks seem completely random."

"Do we know how much the human police know, yet?"

"Wilson is working on it, but at the moment there seems to be very little information available in cyberspace. We're not sure what that means, either. It could be a deliberate attempt to keep the information out of cyberspace and protect it from hacking, or it could simply be the lead detective is slack with his paperwork or a klutz with computers." Thomas ran a hand through his hair, his agitation quite clear to someone who knew him as well as Benjamin did. "The one bit of good news is that Ronan Deeks is involved. He knows one of the police detectives assigned to the case, so we should be able to learn what the human police know as they discover it. We don't have a hope in hell of containing this situation, but we need to find out what's going on and shut it down quickly."

"I agree," Benjamin said, already wondering how he was going to explain to Skye why he was cutting short what was essentially their honeymoon. If it had been any other case, he would have handed over the mission to his team and trusted them to get it done, but with human victims piling up and their prime objective—protect paranormals from human discovery—being compromised they needed everyone on board.

What the hell were the pixies thinking? They might be indestructible beings, but even they relied on the paranormal community's secrecy for their way of life.

Benjamin glanced over at Samuel, realized they were in agreement, and nodded to Dyson and Thomas. "All right, is everyone back on active duty?"

"Not yet," Thomas said with a grimace. "The new boss is requesting that she have the top three squads at her beck and call. Messengers have been sent to everyone currently on holidays."

"Her *beck and call?*" Samuel asked, clearly not liking the idea. "Who took over?"

"Cassandra Lipton," Dyson said with a tight smile. Dyson and Cassandra had history—ancient history—if Benjamin's memory served him well. He hoped like hell that it wasn't going to cause trouble for his squad. It wasn't unusual to find a woman or two on the PUP teams, but it had been a very long time since any of them had taken orders from a female. If nothing else it was going to be an interesting adjustment period.

"Okay, give us a couple of hours to explain to Skye."

Dyson and Thomas nodded, and a moment later seemed to step through an invisible doorway and disappear.

Skye spoke as soon as she saw their faces. "It's okay, I can go stay with my sister," she said trying to smile bravely. "Jennifer won't mind putting up with me for a while."

"Is that what you want?" Samuel asked quietly, studying her face closely.

"This isn't about what I want," Skye said still with that overly bright smile. "You guys have a job to do and it would be far easier without me tagging along."

"Actually," Benjamin said, pulling the woman he loved into his arms, "we were wondering if maybe you'd consider joining the squad."

"Joining the squad? What as? A cheerleader?"

She squeaked as Samuel's large hand connected with her bottom. "No, smart-ass. We mean as a fully trained member of the team."

"Seriously?" she asked in an excited voice.

"You'd have to do a crash course in weapons and defensive training, and you'll probably spend the first couple years doing the paperwork. Most squad members learn on the job, kind of like an apprenticeship, so it wouldn't be like you were getting preferential treatment or anything. We'd insist, of course, that you be assigned permanently to our squad, but otherwise your training would be like anyone else's."

"Seriously?" she asked again with a wide smile. "I can actually do something with my life? I don't have to sit on my ass waiting for you two to save the world over and over? I can actually help?"

Benjamin couldn't help the silly grin that covered his face. Without even realizing it, she'd already proven in the past few months that she was more than capable of being a valued member of their squad. She was smart, quick thinking, intelligent, and reasonable. What more could they ask of a new recruit?

"Yes, baby girl," Benjamin said as he gathered the woman into his arms. Samuel pressed against her back, trapping her between them. "As long as it's what you want, then we'll make it happen."

"I love you," she whispered, reaching up to press a kiss to his lips and then turning slightly to press one to Samuel's mouth. "How long before we need to report in?"

Samuel leaned in and whispered all the things they had time for before they needed to leave. Skye laughed, wriggled out of their combined embrace, and raced toward their room on the second floor. "Gotta catch me first," she said, almost breathless with laughter.

And as they chased her into the room and gathered her once more in their embrace, Benjamin realized a truth he'd not noticed until now. Despite a rewarding career, despite having friends all around him, despite enjoying the first two hundred and three years of his life, now, he was truly happy. Now, he was truly living.

He may not have planned to create a vampire that night, but it was without a doubt the best decision he'd ever made.

THE END

WWW.ABBYBLAKE.BLOGSPOT.COM

Ménage Everlasting

Demon's
EMBRACE

ABBY
BLAKE

PUP SQUAD
ALPHA
2

DEMON'S EMBRACE

PUP Squad Alpha 2

ABBY BLAKE
Copyright © 2012

Prologue

Officer Dave Jenkins threw the file down and rubbed his tired eyes. Three murders in two days and they still had no idea how the victims had died. The only thing they had in common was their age, all twenty-seven, their sex, all female, and the way they'd died, all somehow burned.

Even the coroner, a man with over forty years' experience, had never seen anything like this.

All of the women had died as if they'd somehow been put in a giant microwave. There had been no obvious struggle, no fingerprints, no blood drops or foreign DNA of any kind. Just a dead woman burned from the inside out.

Even their circumstances had been different. One had been single, unemployed, and died at home. One had been a mother of three young children and had died in her car. And the third had been a workaholic lawyer and had died at her desk. None of it made sense.

Dave slammed his hands on the table in frustration, dislodging the pile of file folders in the process and dumping their contents on the floor. Growling at his own frustrated behavior, he bent to gather the scattered papers. A photocopy of one of the women's driver's licenses caught his attention, and he lifted it to look more closely. The date of her birth seemed vaguely familiar, and he wracked his brain for an explanation. He lifted the other two files into his hand and searched for the women's birthdays. He found exactly the same day, month, and year for each victim.

Excited to have found something the three women had in common, and maybe a direction to take the investigation in, Dave gathered the files and headed into his boss's office. At least they might have a way to identify the next potential victim. Half an hour later their team was working on a list of women born in the area on that day twenty-seven years ago.

But as the excitement of a break in the case seeped away, a niggling suspicion wound through his brain. He quickly reached for the phone and dialed home. His wife answered on the second ring.

"Kate, honey, when's my sister's birthday?"

"January twelfth," she answered indulgently. He was always forgetting things like that. "You didn't miss it this year. Remember, we took her to dinner and you tried to set her up with that old army buddy of yours. Even I could see that was a disaster waiting to happen. I mean, seriously, what were you thinking?"

"Kate, I need to go. I'll explain later."

He immediately dialed his sister's number but hung up before she could answer. How was he supposed to explain, over the phone, that she was possibly a serial killer's next victim? Instead, he grabbed his cell phone, scrolled down to a number he hadn't used since before Kali's last birthday, and waited impatiently as the phone rang and rang and rang.

Chapter One

Ronan Deeks was a hard man to find. He did that deliberately. Anyone who truly wanted to talk to him would leave a message, and if he wanted to, he'd call them back. When the phone rang, he didn't bother to stop his workout—it was his favorite part of the day after all—but he did turn down the music volume so he could listen to the answering machine as it clicked on.

The deep voice was familiar and one he hadn't heard in quite a long time, but it was the tone of underlying fear that caught his attention. Dave Jenkins was not an easy man to frighten, but it was clear in his voice that he was very worried for his sister's safety. Ronan turned off the treadmill, grabbed a towel, and snatched up the phone before Dave could hang up.

"Dave," he said calmly. Whatever had his friend rattled seemed to be serious.

"Thank God," Dave said fervently. "I need your help. All the victims share a birthday. Kali's birthday—day, month, and year. We're working on a possible list right now, but I need you to protect her while I track down this asshole. I'll pay you whatever it takes."

There was no way Dave would be able to afford Ronan's services on his cop's salary, and Ronan had no intention of charging him anyway, but it was a measure of the man's very real worry for his sister.

"Hang on. Back up a minute. What victims? Which asshole?"

The explanation was chilling.

Even if the birth dates were a coincidence—and with all three victims being born on that particular day it seemed unlikely—

statistically speaking, there would be many, many female babies born on that day also. The chances of Dave's sister, Kali, being one of the killer's targets was probably slim but certainly not something either of them was willing to overlook.

But it was the manner of death that convinced him that this was no ordinary serial killer. As he gathered what he would need for this mission, he dialed a number he knew from memory. He nearly laughed at the grumpy greeting but got straight to the point. "Remember that favor you owe me, asshole? I'm calling it in."

* * * *

Kali Jenkins watched with glee as her aim proved accurate and the Angry Bird destroyed the final stone tower and dumped the last little pig on the ground before it disappeared. Finally, after millions of attempts—okay, maybe fifteen—that level was done. She pressed the button to continue, intending only to look at the next level before putting her phone away and getting back to work, but the level looked too interesting, and she decided to try just once.

Ten or twelve attempts later she was interrupted from her little war against green piggies when someone knocked on her door. She glanced at the clock, surprised to realize more than a half hour had passed since she'd decided to take a break. Hell, being her own boss really had its drawbacks sometimes.

She plastered on a smile and opened the door, hoping that whoever stood on the other side wouldn't take forever to get rid of. But the annoying, oversized, and very familiar Neanderthal pushed past her and stepped into her foyer without even saying hello.

"What do you want?" she demanded, hands on her hips, foot tapping in annoyance.

"I want you to close the door, lock it, and then sit down so we can talk."

"Look, you and me," she said, waving her hands between them, "have nothing to talk about."

"Turns out that's not exactly true."

She rolled her eyes, stomped her foot in annoyance, and considered using her phone for something besides playing Angry Birds—like maybe calling the police.

The thought was only half formed when her brother stepped through the open doorway, gave her an annoyed look, and then turned to lock it like Ronan had ordered when he first walked in. Of course, simply the fact that Ronan had ordered her to do it in the first place was a good enough reason for her to leave it open. That and the fact she wanted the obnoxious man out of her house.

Seriously, one horrible, tragic, pathetic double date with her brother and his wife should have made certain that neither of them wanted to be in the same room ever again.

"What do you want?" she asked her brother. Maybe she'd get a straight answer out of him.

"I want you to listen to Ronan. He's going to keep you safe."

The words "what the fuck?" were bouncing around her head, but since she tried not to swear in front of her big brother, she swallowed them and turned her gaze on Ronan. It didn't help her anger levels that the man was still good looking, hard in all the right places, and built like any woman's wildest dream.

Just because she'd fantasized about him a time or two—okay, at least a couple dozen—it didn't mean she wanted to put up with the man's obnoxious personality. Hell, if he could maybe get a personality transplant, he might actually be the perfect man.

But none of her mental meanderings explained why her brother and his annoying army buddy were standing in the middle of her living room. Through clenched teeth she asked for an explanation one more time. "What makes you think I'm not safe?"

"It's just a precaution," Dave said, suddenly acting like nothing was wrong. Again the words "what the fuck?" where bouncing around her head, and at this rate they were liable to bounce right out of her mouth, brother or not.

"A precaution for what?" Her jaw was starting to ache from the effort of holding back her temper. It had been obvious when her brother walked in that he was very agitated about something, so the nonchalant act wasn't fooling her.

"I've got to go," Dave said and moved to press a kiss to her forehead. "Listen to Ronan. He'll keep you safe."

"Uh-huh," she said, not wanting to commit to that course of action. Seriously, the guy didn't even smell pleasant. Had he come straight from the gym? God, she hoped so, because having a man who smelled like that all the time was seriously going to overtax her potpourri. And, well okay, it wasn't exactly an unpleasant odor, more of a clean, sweaty, hot man smell rather than a full-on stink, but this was her house. Shouldn't she have the final say in what smells— delicious or otherwise—should be allowed in?

With a final nod in Ronan's direction, Dave left, pulled the door behind him, and used his own key to lock her deadbolt. She turned to Ronan, put her hands on her hips, and issued her demand. "Explain."

He shrugged.

She growled low in her throat and wished she had the physical strength to toss him out of her house. Maybe if she'd gone to the gym instead of playing games on her cell phone she would have been able. She glanced at the man-mountain with legs as thick as tree trunks and dismissed her fanciful thinking. It wouldn't have mattered how many times she visited the gym, she'd need three of her just to shift his stubborn ass.

"Are you hungry?" he asked as he headed toward the phone in her kitchen. "I'll order something for delivery. What do you feel like?"

"I feel like I want a straight fucking answer."

He gave her that arrogant look she remembered from their "date"—if that disastrous dinner and what happened afterward could even be called that—and wanted to smack him upside the head. Shit.

So much for her claims of being a pacifist. One minute in this guy's company and she really, *really* wanted to hit something.

She doubted she was the only one to feel the urges he inspired. He even looked like he was about to say something that would really piss her off when the front door chimed.

What the hell was this? Grand *fucking* Central?

"Stay there," Ronan said as he headed toward the front door. The only thing that made her not do the opposite of what he said was the memory of her brother's agitation. He'd been very worried, and whatever was going on, she wasn't silly enough to discount the seriousness of it. "Good timing," Ronan said to whoever was at the door. A moment later he walked past her and headed toward the hallway. Just before he stepped out of the room, he turned back. "This is Alex. Do what he says. I'm going for a shower."

Flabbergasted didn't even begin to describe how she was feeling at that moment.

She turned to the man, correction, the stranger in her kitchen and wondered what the hell to do now.

Chapter Two

Alex Clements winked at the pretty redhead standing there with her mouth open and tried not to smile too widely. He'd seen that expression before. Only Ronan could inspire such speechless anger. The guy was like a bull in the proverbial china shop. Wherever he went, he left behind a trail of pissed-off women.

Fortunately, Alex prided himself on his ability to charm even the most annoyed of females. Although, working with Ronan on this assignment just might stretch his ability to the limit.

"Is he always like that?"

"Pretty much," Alex agreed with a smile. He held his hand out. "I'm Alex Clements."

"Uh-huh," she said, not bothering to give her name or shake his hand. He quirked an eyebrow at her attitude, but she simply locked her jaw and stared him down. If she knew how much he was aroused by her belligerent behavior, she probably wouldn't have been so obvious. He wasn't sure what that said about him, but he'd always enjoyed a challenge. And this lovely, fire-tempered, redheaded beauty was pushing all of his buttons.

He dragged in a deep breath, let it out slowly, and tried to remind himself that he was on an assignment. Granted, it wasn't his usual type of gig, but he did owe the big guy a favor.

"Did Ronan explain what's going on?"

She quirked her eyebrow in exactly the same manner he'd done. He couldn't help but laugh at her style. Goddess, he loved a woman with an attitude.

"I'll take that as a no," he said as he leaned against the kitchen counter and tried to hide the fact he was checking her out from head to toe. The woman truly was his type—tall, curvy, stubborn. She was almost his perfect match. Well, except for the being human part. "Look, I don't have all the facts yet either, but some cop that Ronan knows asked him to look after you. He said something about a serial killer and you maybe being his next victim."

"Serial killer?" She looked a bit pale, but she managed to stay upright and narrow her eyes at him in anger. Good, right now that emotion would do her more good than fear or hysteria.

"Like I said, I'm not sure of the details, but this cop—your brother?—truly believes you are on this serial killer's list and wants you to be safe."

"So he hired me two bodyguards?"

"Well, technically, he only hired Ronan, but I owe the big guy a favor or three, so here I am."

"What, he didn't think he could protect little ole me by himself?" She made the question sound like a snarky insult, and Alex had to laugh at her moxie. Hell, there weren't many people—human or otherwise—on the planet who would deliberately insult Ronan Deeks. She didn't even flinch when the man himself came back into the kitchen wearing only a towel.

"That's right, princess. It's going to take two of us to keep your stubborn little ass out of trouble."

"Little?" she asked, sounding startled, but then she shook her head slightly as if realizing Ronan's description of her butt, small or otherwise, wasn't the most important part of that statement. "What do we know about this serial killer? Did Dave explain why he thinks I'm a target?"

"Only that the first three victims all shared your birthday."

"Seriously? That's it? That they shared my birthday. There are five million people living in this town. That means that there are what? Thirteen, fourteen thousand people who share my birthday in this area alone."

"Yes, but the victims were all female and all born in the same year. They were all twenty-seven. Just like you, so that changes the numbers considerably. Correct me if my math is wrong, but that brings it closer to one hundred or so."

"That's still a pretty big number," the woman said with just the slightest hint of fear.

Ronan stepped closer, crowding her with his big body. He touched her face almost reverently. It was an interesting move from a man who usually held people—women especially—at arm's length.

"It's a number small enough to make your brother worry, princess. So let me and Alex do our jobs, and we promise to keep you safe."

Her gaze flickered to Alex and then back to Ronan. "Okay," she said quietly, "but only because I don't want my brother to waste energy worrying about me."

"No problem, princess. Your brother is the only reason I'm here. As soon as they catch this serial killer, I'll be out of your hair, and you'll never have to see me again."

"Good," she said with just a little bit too much vehemence.

Despite the insult apparent in their words, Alex could read their body language very clearly. There was a physical attraction between them and, even if neither of them acknowledged it, maybe even an emotional connection. Interesting.

"Okay," Alex said, trying to stay focused on their mission. Safety first and all that. "I understand you work from home. Is that correct?"

"Yes," the woman said with a puzzled frown. "What's your point?"

Oh, he really liked this one.

"It would be far easier to have this conversation if I knew your name."

Her eyes narrowed with anger, but she managed to grind out through clenched teeth, "Kali Jenkins."

"Ah, a beautiful name for a beautiful woman," Alex said with a smirk in Ronan's direction. He was so focused on Ronan's reaction that he almost missed Kali's eye roll. She truly was something special, and if he didn't stop teasing her, she was going to look down and see the erection trying to break free from his pants. "Okay, my point is that if you work from home, you can essentially work from anywhere that has an Internet connection. Correct?"

"Well, kind of. I mean, maybe for a short time, but…well, it's not good to…um…" She trailed off as if she were looking for a bullshit excuse, before Ronan stepped in and started barking orders. Well, maybe barking was a harsh description, but he sure could use a few hints on how to deal with a stubborn lady. Although, come to think of it, the guy could probably just use some lessons in dealing with people overall. For a human being, he really sucked at dealing with other humans.

"Please excuse my dumbass friend's rudeness," Alex said as he stepped closer to Kali and tried not to pull her into his arms. Goddess, he'd never quite found it so hard to resist a human before. "Kali, we have a safe house a couple hours' drive from here. We can help pack your things. Take as much as you'll need for two weeks, and then we'll make a decision after that."

"Two weeks?" she asked in a higher-pitched voice than he'd been expecting. Wow, he hoped she didn't do that very often. He tugged on his earlobe in the hopes of stopping his ears from ringing.

"Hopefully, we can have you back here much sooner, but at least with two weeks' worth of stuff you'll be able to continue with your normal routine. You'll just be somewhere else."

"Oh, sure," she said quietly, a hint of vulnerability sneaking through her tough demeanor.

He couldn't help himself. He pulled her into his embrace, smiling when she wrapped her arms around his waist and held on tight. "Like you said, the odds are in your favor. Let's just keep them that way."

She nodded, her head rubbing softly against his chest with her movement. "How long do I have?"

"Five minutes," Ronan growled in a voice rough enough to cut glass. "Move."

* * * *

The angry look she turned on Ronan was exactly the opposite of what he needed. As soon as the words had come out of his mouth, he'd wanted to take them back. He wasn't even sure what had made him go all drill sergeant on her anyway. It couldn't have been jealousy that she'd clung to Alex like he was her last hope, because that would imply that Ronan had feelings for the woman. Which, of course, was ridiculous, because she was nothing like the type of woman he usually dated.

He preferred quiet, biddable beauties who did what he asked without arguing. He liked tall, cool blondes, not fiery redheads curved in all the right places and just looking for the worst moment to explode in temper. He couldn't even imagine dating a woman who questioned his every move and challenged him at every step. He'd probably end up tipping such a difficult woman over his knee and smacking that pert, deliciously curved bottom until she cried out his name and shattered with orgasm.

Nope, he couldn't imagine any of it.

He wrapped the towel tighter around his groin, glanced at the knowing smirk on Alex's face, and then grabbed his bag and headed back into the bathroom. Hell, he wasn't even sure why he'd forgotten to take his stuff in with him in the first place. It's not like he actually wanted her to see, and maybe remember and admire, the hard planes of his chest and abdomen. He was in good shape, but it wasn't like he needed her to notice.

So why then was he disappointed that she continued to hold on to Alex as if the world were coming to an end?

Fortunately that last thought put him back on track. In a way her world was coming to an end. Even after this was all over, it would be difficult to forget that feeling of no longer being safe in her own home. If he could, he'd shield her from it. That's why he was here. He had a job to do. He and Kali had already done and failed the whole "relationship" thing—if the few hours they'd spent together could even be called that—so he had no reason to even consider such unimportant things when he was here to keep her safe. He needed to protect her, not rehash ancient history.

He carefully pulled his jeans over the erection that wouldn't quit, strapped on his weapons, and then headed back into the kitchen in the hopes that Kali and Alex had taken his "five minutes" order seriously and were already packed.

* * * *

Kali finally realized she was clinging to the man like some sort of vine. Sheesh, she'd never been the damsel-in-distress type, so why was she acting it now?

She pushed gently against Alex's chest, and after a heart-stopping moment of hesitation he let her leave his embrace.

"Sorry," she whispered, quite embarrassed by her behavior. She'd met the man all of two minutes ago.

"Don't be," Alex said with a genuine smile. "Anytime you want a cuddle, darlin', I'm your man."

She nodded, relaxing slightly despite his flirty demeanor. He probably spoke to all of their clients like that. Hell, with a work partner like Ronan, Alex would need all the charm he could muster.

As if she'd conjured him with just the thought, Ronan marched back into the kitchen dressed in jeans and a casual sweater and looking more handsome than any mere mortal had a right to. With a face as fine looking as his, it was almost criminal that he would have the body to match. No man deserved to be that lucky. Except that, well, considering his abrasive personality, maybe there was some sort of cosmic balance at play. He could attract the girls. He just couldn't keep them.

Appalled at her nasty thoughts, Kali turned to the kitchen table she used as a work station and tried to decide what she would need to be able to work while she was away. She heard a sound in her hallway and turned to see both men exchange a look before Alex headed toward the front door and Ronan wrapped an arm around her and dragged her toward the bedroom. Annoyed at his heavy-handed response to what was probably only her brother returning—he was the only one with a key after all—she tried to tell Ronan to lighten up. Of course that would have been much easier if he hadn't placed his big hand over her mouth. She gave him a look that should have fried him on the spot, but he just shook his head and held her closer.

"We need to go. Now!" Alex said as he stalked into the room, grabbed her hand in one of his, and placed the other on Ronan's shoulder. What happened after that was still a blur ten minutes later, but she was sure she never, ever wanted it to happen again.

* * * *

Ronan shook his head for about the millionth time since they'd landed. Well, landed probably wasn't the best description for arriving at their destination by some sort of demon-hoodoo-voodoo-whatsit-type transport. It always left him feeling like the day *after* he'd been shot. Fuck.

Poor Kali hadn't fared any better. She'd been green since the moment they'd arrived and hadn't even bothered to demand an explanation. He had no doubt that conversation was coming. It was just a measure of how ill she must feel that she hadn't started it yet. She'd curled up into a ball on the sofa, and Ronan wished he could do the same, maybe even beside her, or curled around her, or lying over her.

His cock stirred, and he groaned at the inconvenient timing of his imagination.

"Where are we?" he asked Alex, trying desperately to get his mind back onto business and away from the vulnerable-looking woman lying on the sofa.

"My place," Alex answered easily. "I figured that, considering what found us, it was best to get as far away as possible."

Ronan glanced at Kali's sleeping form and lowered his voice a little more. "What found us?"

"A pixie," Alex said with an exaggerated shudder. "Nasty little bitches."

"Seriously?" Ronan asked, half expecting Alex to laugh and tell him what they were really running from. When Alex just nodded, Ronan couldn't help himself. He had to know. "What happened?"

Alex shrugged. "Basically, I recognized her. She recognized me. I incinerated the bitch's ass before she could incinerate mine."

"You did what?"

It wasn't that he didn't believe Alex—he was a handy ally in a fight—but it seemed a rather extreme reaction when what they really could have used was someone to interrogate.

"Don't worry," Alex said with a wink. "Pixies recover from incineration. Haven't you ever heard of pixie dust? But I needed her to be out of action long enough to get us here. If she'd been conscious, she would have been able to follow." Ronan was sure his head was spinning from all of this new information. Yeah, he'd been friends with Alex for a long time, but he'd always tried to ignore the fact that the guy wasn't human.

But then Alex glanced over at Kali and suddenly became very serious. "You wanted to know what could burn a human from the inside out—our little visitor was more than capable. I'm afraid your cop friend's instincts were right on the money. Whatever is going on, the attacks definitely aren't random, and they sure as hell aren't the work of a human serial killer."

"So what do we do now?" Ronan asked. He really had hoped that Dave's reaction had just been a big brother overreacting to a possible threat to his sister, but the fact that Alex had exposed his nonhuman nature to Kali was a pretty good indicator that they were in deep shit.

"Unfortunately, now we need to get PUP Squad Alpha involved. They're all on leave at the moment, but that might be a good thing in this instance." He glanced over at Kali, a frown marring his features. "The pixies are good assassins, but they usually work for a price. I doubt they're the ones actually ordering the attacks. My biggest worry is figuring out who we can trust outside of my squad. The Ruling Body was set up to protect paranormals from humans. Not the other way around. It's likely they'll only get involved if the assassinations threaten to expose the paranormal community."

"What about the date? Kali's birthday…it seems to be a significant part of what's happening."

"Not sure about that one," Alex said as he headed over to a panel in the wall, "but I have a few people I can ask." He fiddled with some strange-looking dials and then closed the cover. "I've set the protection wards so that no one—not even me—can slip travel into or out of the house. Anyone wanting to visit will have to slip outside and find their way in."

"Wait, back up a minute." Ronan rubbed a hand over his eyes and silently gave himself the "you can handle anything" speech. "Protection wards? Aren't they supposed to be magical? That looked more like a high-tech security system."

Alex's lips curved into that annoying grin that made Ronan want to hit something.

"That's the thing about magic," Alex said with another wink, "eventually some scientist comes along and explains it." He nodded at the panel on the wall. "Far easier these days to create a field to stop slip travelers. As long as that's active you won't come face-to-face with any paranormals inside the house." He glanced at Ronan's semiautomatic handgun and grinned once more. "That thing'll hurt most, but in case you find yourself with something a little harder to maim, I'll leave you some demon shots."

"Some what?"

"Demon shots," Alex said as he handed over a handful of rather ordinary-looking bullets. "Basically, these will incinerate an intruder much the same way I incinerated that pixie. It won't work on fire demons and will only give you a few moments of escape time with a pixie, but pretty much everyone else is toast."

"Uh, okay," Ronan said, trying not to sound like he had no clue what was going on. "Want to tell me what a pixie looks like? You know, so I know the difference between dead and dust."

"Easy," Alex said with another laugh, "pixies look like seven-year-olds selling cookies. Other paranormals don't."

"What the hell?" Ronan was seriously wondering why he'd answered the phone this morning, but a quick glance at Kali still sleeping on the sofa brought things back into sharp focus.

"I'll be as quick as I can," Alex said as he headed outside. "You should be safe here. And, just so you know, there aren't any seven-year-olds in this area of the world. You see one, shoot first. Don't hesitate."

"Okay," Ronan said with a decisive nod.

He watched through the window as Alex walked about a hundred yards from the house and then seemed somehow to step into an invisible doorway. Rubbing his eyes, Ronan turned back to find Kali awake and staring at him as if he'd grown a second head. Hell, considering the type of day he'd had so far, it was likely to be true.

"What the fuck did you do to me?" she growled as she tried to leap off the sofa and confront him. The only problem was she swooned instead and landed in his arms. He gathered her close, took a seat on the sofa, and waited for her to regain her equilibrium. "Put me down."

"Not until I'm sure you're all right."

"How can I be all right? One minute I'm standing in my kitchen, and then the next thing I know I'm lying on a strange sofa. Where the hell are we?" She rubbed her eyes tiredly. "And what the fuck did you give me? I feel like shit." She cuddled against him even though he was fairly certain she really didn't mean to. "It's not nice to drug an ex. That sort of stalker shit can get you into big trouble. And besides, I'd already agreed to go with you anyway, so why would you knock me out?" Her voice gave away how tired she was, but the ornery woman lifted her head and glanced around the room, her gaze eventually settling on the big glass windows that overlooked a massive tree-filled valley. "And, hey, where the hell are we?"

"You asked that already," Ronan said with a smile as he eased her head back against his chest. It felt too good to hold her, especially at the moment when she seemed disinclined to fight him on it.

"And yet I still don't have an answer," she said in a grumpy voice, even though she slumped against him even more.

"We're at Alex's place."

"How long was I out?"

He considered lying and letting her think that they'd drugged her, but in light of what they seemed to be facing, it was probably dangerous to keep her in the dark. "You were only unconscious for a few minutes."

"So we're not far from my home then?"

"In a manner of speaking," he said carefully. Now that he'd made the decision he really didn't know how to go about explaining it. The words *"Hey, doll, did you know the world is full of paranormal creatures?"* probably wouldn't help.

"Where's Alex?" she asked with such affection in her voice that she managed to piss him off once more. Hell, jealous much?

"He's gone to speak to some of his contacts. He should be back soon."

"Oh, okay," she said as she shuffled slightly in his lap. He managed to bite back the groan as she dragged her beautiful ass against his hard cock, but she noticed the hard rod anyway. She looked like she was about to give him a few choice words, but then something caught her attention, and she looked over at the window.

"Where did that kid come from?"

Terror filled him as Ronan followed her gaze and saw exactly what she was looking at. Fuck, Alex hadn't been kidding when he'd said pixies looked like seven-year-olds selling cookies. Before he could react, Alex came into sight, almost like he stepped around a corner without there actually having been a corner to step around. He immediately blasted the pixie with what looked a lot like a flamethrower but without the hardware, rushed past the burning body as it crumbled into dust, and came into the room.

"Time to go," he said as he twisted the dial on the wall panel, placed his hands on them both, and then made the world spin out of control once more.

Chapter Three

"Don't," Kali said, swallowing hard, "ever, *ever* do that again."

"Cell phone, Kali? Where is it?"

"Jacket pocket," she managed to force past her chattering teeth. It felt like someone had put her in a paint shaker. Her head pounded, her stomach threatened revolt, and every ounce of energy she'd owned had completely fled. Even her eyes refused to focus. Kali registered her phone being taken from her jacket. The smell of melting plastic and hot metal a moment later was confusing, but she couldn't really identify its source.

Ronan still held her, but he was also shaking with fatigue. From a strange type of sitting position he fell onto his ass on the floor and managed to take her down with him. He stretched out, and she lay sprawled across him, unable to move without feeling like she would lose her lunch.

"I agree with Kali," Ronan said as he wrapped his arms around her and shifted her to a more comfortable spot. "No more slip travel. Twice in one day is very unpleasant. I think another one just might kill me."

"Nah," Alex said from somewhere above them. It sounded like he was moving around. "You just need to find your sea legs. It gets easier."

Considering that she felt way worse than she had the first time, she found that hard to believe. "Wait! 'Slip travel'? What the fuck is that?"

"It's the way fire demons travel. Quite convenient really."

"Fire demons?" Okay, now she knew for certain that they'd broken something in her brain. Fire demons? Slip travel? Incinerated seven-year-olds? There was no way she was sane. Maybe she was already locked in a rubber room.

Alex pressed something into her hand. "Eat this. I promise it will make you feel better."

She squinted at the salt-encrusted cracker and really wanted to roll her eyes. She resisted, of course. Her headache was bad enough as it was. Unable to form any type of smartass reply, Kali lifted the cracker to her mouth and nibbled on the corner instead. It was really, really salty. Great, now she felt nauseous *and* thirsty.

Kali could hear Ronan munching away, the chewing sound rather noisy with her ear pressed against his chest. She shuffled sideways, intending only to climb off the man—she really shouldn't have stayed there in the first place—but Alex lifted her into his arms and settled her on his lap as he sat on some sort of bench.

Feeling just a little less woozy than she had a moment ago, Kali managed to keep her eyes open long enough to look around. "Where are we this time?" They seemed to be in some sort of gym.

"My place," Ronan said as he managed to lift himself off the floor and stay upright with minimal swaying. "Good choice." He nodded to Alex and then turned and headed out of the room.

"I'm crazy, aren't I?" she whispered to Alex. "I would have sworn I saw you attack a seven-year-old with flames from your fingers. I'm really in a hospital psych ward or something, aren't I?"

"Sorry to disappoint you, darlin', but you really did see what you thought you saw." He touched her face softly but shook his head as a grin formed on his lips. "Well, except for the seven-year-old. That was actually a pixie assassin, and unfortunately she'll recover from that and come after you again. Of course, that's *if* she can find us. I think she got lucky at my place, but I destroyed your cell phone just in case she was using modern technology to track you."

"A pixie assassin?" Her voice was way higher in pitch than she liked—and she'd get to the part about her destroyed cell phone in a moment—but pixie assassins? He was joking, right? "Aren't pixies supposed to be cute and nice and...*not* assassins and...I don't know...not real?"

"Sorry to disappoint you, but despite their positive—and very much undeserved—reputations, pixies aren't nice, aren't cute, and really do assassinate people. Well, they usually stick to paranormal-type people to assassinate, but I can assure you they are very real."

"Oh," Kali said as her headache throbbed just a little more. Maybe *she* wasn't the only crazy one in this room.

"Now fire demons, on the other hand," Alex continued, "have a bad reputation, yet we've never done anything to deserve it. I mean, yeah, we can incinerate anything we want to with our bare hands, but it's not like we go around doing it all the time. And hey, what's with the Halloween BS? I don't look like a guy with red skin, yellow horns, and a tail, do I?"

She shook her head and wondered how long she was going to get to stay in crazy-land.

"You still going on about needing a better publicist?" Ronan said as he strode back into the room. He didn't seem the least bit affected by whatever had knocked him on his ass a few minutes ago. Lucky bastard. Although, if Kali were honest with herself, she'd admit that she was staying in Alex's arms more for her own reasons now. The headache wasn't nearly as bad as it had been, and the nausea was mostly gone. But she snuggled just a little closer when she saw jealousy flash across Ronan's features. It lasted but a moment, yet she knew exactly what she'd seen.

Served him right. One disastrous date and pity sex five months ago didn't mean they were involved. It didn't even make them friends.

The saddest part about that was she'd been the one on the receiving end of the pity sex. Pathetic. Sad *and* pathetic and something she'd never wanted to be reminded of. She made a mental note to smack her big brother upside the head next time she saw him. It was all his fault after all. He'd set up the date. He'd introduced them. He and his wife had left her alone with the man. He…Okay, her brother hadn't suggested she ask Ronan to take her to bed in a pathetically weak and drunken moment, but he was to blame for the rest of the mess.

Ronan watched her with eyes that saw way more than she wanted him to see and then seemed to shake himself and get back on topic. "Are we safe here?" he asked Alex.

"I would suggest one more slip." Kali actually shuddered at the thought. She might not believe her eyes or her ears at the moment, but there was no way she wanted to experience again whatever it was that had caused the nausea. Alex pulled her closer and pressed a kiss to the top of her head. "But since neither of you seem up to it, we should probably take your car. We can head for the safe house. It shouldn't have been compromised."

"Did you learn any news from your squad?"

"I did," Alex said with a nod as he pulled her closer. Somehow that didn't make her feel any better.

"Okay," Ronan said as he headed out into what seemed to be a hallway, "we move out in five minutes. Grab whatever you think we might need. I'll be back in a minute."

Kali didn't quite know what to do. Even when they'd been at her home the only thing she'd thought to pack was technology. But if they were tracking her by her cell phone signal, chances were they'd be able to trace her location the moment she connected to the Internet. It seemed really strange to be thinking this way but, almost like she was lost in a thick fog, her life just seemed surreal. If Ronan said he was here to protect her, and Alex said he was a fire demon and that pixies were nasty little assassins, who was she to argue?

Seriously, who *was* she to argue?

Willing to go on a little faith—at least until she had proof otherwise—Kali let Alex lead her around the house as he gathered "stuff" for while they'd be away. She wasn't even sure what he was collecting. She was just really glad that he held on to her hand while he did it.

"Ready?" Ronan asked as he came into the room. She must have been wearing a shell-shocked expression because he gathered her in his arms and held her close. "I know this is a lot to take in, Kali, but I assure you you're safe with us." She nodded against his chest and held on tight. It wasn't like her to be so needy, but she gave herself permission to lean on these men…just this once.

* * * *

Alex happily sat in the back of the car with Kali. He knew it was driving Ronan nuts, but at this point he didn't really care. If they needed to slip travel urgently, it was far faster if he was already touching the woman. And besides, despite her human status, Alex found himself quite happy to hold the beautiful redhead while she was in such a compliant and snuggly mood.

He had no doubt that would change once they got to the safe house and she gained some perspective. Unfortunately, the information he needed to share with them both wasn't going to help any of them get back to their normal lives.

They'd barely made it out of the driveway before Ronan gave him the "start talking" look.

"It would seem that Kali's birthday was a rather big event in the paranormal community. One of the Oracles was murdered that same day." He was going to explain what an Oracle was, but both humans nodded as if they understood and so he continued. "When an Oracle dies she sends her entire knowledge to the next female child who is born. Since there weren't any paranormal communities in the area where she was murdered, it was assumed that the information was lost."

"But someone has decided it went to a human child?"

"That's my guess."

"So they're killing every female born on my birthday?" Kali asked in a small voice. Alex nodded and wanted to pull Kali closer, but of course the stubborn redhead chose that moment to find the attitude he so admired. "We have to help them. We have to warn them."

"Your brother is working on it, but we're still talking a hundred or more potential victims here. There's no way we can help them all," Ronan said from the front seat. Alex had known him long enough to sense the despair behind that statement. No matter how many innocent lives Ronan managed to protect, it had always been the ones he couldn't save that stuck with him.

"There has to be a way to narrow it down. I mean...we have to know something more. Surely there's something missing. What are we missing?" Kali's gaze swung between both men, but almost as if a light bulb had switched on in her head, her eyes settled on Alex. "How long does it take for the information to be passed on from a dying Oracle? Is it something gradual or is it instant? Would there be a specific window of time for the baby to be born? I mean...hell, I'm not sure what I mean...I just...is it possible that they are targeting women born at a specific time on that day?"

"That's quite likely," Alex answered as theories started forming in his brain. "I'm not exactly an expert on Oracles, but I believe the information transfer is almost instantaneous at the moment of death."

"So," Kali said, looking thoughtful, "if whoever is looking for these women knows that, they'd be targeting the ones who'd been born the exact moment of the Oracle's death."

"Give or take a couple of minutes to allow for slight differences in clock settings," Ronan added with a nod.

"Okay, so if we know the specific time the Oracle died, then we can narrow down the list of women who need protecting."

Alex ground his teeth together, not wanting to upset Kali but needing to give her the bad news anyway. "Trouble is I don't know her actual moment of death. I doubt anyone knows, except maybe her murderer."

"We don't need to know it," Kali said, looking maybe just a little bit excited. "Call my brother. He'll have access to the victims' birth certificates showing the time of birth. I know it's a long shot, but it's a fair assumption that whoever wants the Oracle's supposed recipient dead is also the person who wanted the Oracle dead." Alex nodded in agreement. "So they would be the one person who would know her time of death. Why send assassins to kill hundreds when they can narrow it down to a handful?"

"Good point," Ronan said as he pulled the car to a stop. "Don't scare Dave. He doesn't know anything about paranormals. If we need to tell him, I'd rather it be before he sees you appear out of nowhere."

Alex nodded, pressed a kiss to Kali's lips, and slipped straight to her brother's office across town.

* * * *

Ronan ground his teeth, annoyed at the soft smile that graced Kali's face. "Climb into the front seat," he growled even though it was supposed to be a suggestion, not an order. He would have tried to smile but was worried that it would come off as more of an aggressive show of teeth instead of the reassurance he was hoping for. Kali moved quickly, climbing over the seat just like he'd asked rather than stepping out of the car. He spared a moment for her to grab her seat belt before setting the car in motion once more.

"He's gone to talk to Dave?" she asked quietly, but before he could say anything, she seemed to answer her unasked question. "Oh, right, no cell phones." She glanced around the ordinary-looking streets of the small town they were passing through and then turned her attention back to him. "Are we vulnerable without Alex?"

Great. Fucking great. It wasn't that he begrudged Alex's rather handy skill set, but it pissed him off that Kali would think he needed Alex's help to protect her. He was more than capable of holding his own against paranormals. It was how he and Alex had met in the first place. Granted, he hadn't come up against pixies before, but that shouldn't be a problem anymore, especially now that he had a whole box of demon shots. He could very literally stand over the ashes of a pixie, wait for her to reform, and shoot her again. He also had an inkling that a sticky substance like paint lacquer or the spray glue he'd tucked under his seat would slow the pixie's reformation down, if not stop it all together.

He shook his head when he imagined Alex's reaction to that. The trouble with paranormals was that they lived so long they forgot to think outside the box. Alex was one of the more progressive members of his species, having embraced human science and modern technology, but the majority of his people still clung to the past. It was amazing how few of them had any clue of the destructive range of weapons humans had developed in the past hundred years. Ronan could still see the shocked expression on his attacker's face when he'd shot the massive creature with a bazooka. He didn't enjoy killing anything, but he sure as hell wasn't going to stand by while a creature from his nightmares tried to snack on him and his squad.

"Ronan?" Kali asked quietly. "Ronan, are you all right?"

"I'm fine, Kali." He glanced in her direction and saw the concern on her face. "I'm sorry. I was just..." He trailed off, not really wanting to explain his trip down memory lane. It had been a life-changing experience. Although, he'd met Alex that day and they'd been friends ever since, so it hadn't all been bad. "If we keep the car moving, nothing paranormal can *slip* in. They need two stationary points to travel that way. There's nothing between us and the safe house now, so we have no reason to stop."

"Oh." She didn't really sound convinced, and he glanced in her direction before turning his attention back to the road.

"Oh?" he asked, hoping she would elaborate. This couldn't be easy for her. Not only was she learning about paranormals for the first time, but she got to spend time with a man she'd already rejected months ago and a stranger who just happened to be a fire demon with a penchant for seducing pretty ladies. Although, come to think of it, Alex usually restricted his flirting to females of the paranormal persuasion.

"I'm just…" Kali twisted her fingers in her lap, and Ronan felt his apprehension level increase. Despite their short acquaintance five months ago, he would have sworn that she didn't have any emotional "tells." She'd worn what he'd considered a polite and friendly expression for most of their time together, but it hadn't given him any clues on what she'd been thinking. It had only been when she was in the throes of arousal and screaming in orgasm that he'd seen the passionate woman underneath. How was it that months after she'd fled his bed he still wanted a chance to do it better? To make up for whatever he'd done wrong? She was just one woman in a long line of disastrous relationships. Why was this one special?

Kali took a deep breath and started again. "I'm just sorry that you got dragged into this mess. I mean…it…it can't be easy for you to have to deal with me after the way I embarrassed myself on my birthday."

"The way you…" He bit back the words, trying to figure out what she meant. She'd been lovely—a perfect date and an unexpected gift as a bed partner. They'd spent most of the night exploring each other, and even now he could feel his cock rising at the memories. Granted, he'd managed to say and do just about everything wrong on their "date," but the sex had been amazing, and it hadn't been until the morning after that the awkwardness had started.

He wanted to pull the car over and deal with whatever it was that had gone wrong between them five months ago, but the threat of paranormal attack was still very real. He kept his eyes on the road and asked the question he'd wanted an answer to since that day. "Why did you leave?"

"Why did I leave? Are you nuts?" He frowned and gripped the steering wheel tighter. He was about to ask the same question again when she took a deep breath and started talking really fast. "I shouldn't have used you that way. It was wrong and I'm sorry. I'm not usually so needy, but it was my birthday and I was feeling lonely and depressed and…well none of that excuses my behavior. I just…I wanted you to know I was sorry, and even though we're going to have to spend some time together while this shit all gets sorted out that I won't do anything so selfish again."

Hell, if he could stop the car, he'd drag her over his knees and smack her ass. And then kiss it better and maybe even roll her over so he could trace his tongue over her pussy, find her clit, and suckle on the hard nub until she came screaming his name.

Fuck. She thought she'd "used" him? He hadn't just been a willing participant. He'd wanted in her bed almost from the moment he'd met her. He'd sensed something, felt something…hell, he couldn't describe it, but it was almost as if they belonged together. He may have seemed reluctant when she'd first suggested that he take her to his bed, but that had only been because he'd wanted more than a quick fuck from her. If he'd known she was going to run, he would have tied the woman to his bed long before the morning had come.

He stayed quiet, unsure what to say. He'd fucked this up once already. Clearly, telling her in words was not one of his strengths. He'd always preferred action over talking anyway.

They eventually turned onto the dirt track that would take them to the safe house, and Ronan was glad to see Alex waiting for them. It would give him a chance to do what he needed to do without having to worry about keeping his guard up in case of attack. For a few moments he fully intended to show Kali exactly what he'd been thinking five months ago.

Chapter Four

Kali smiled at Alex through the windshield and then turned to open her car door. She almost fell out as it opened from the outside and Ronan offered her his hand. Unsure if her apology was accepted or not, Kali almost yelped when he lifted her straight up and fused his mouth to hers. He used her surprise to thrust his tongue past her teeth and reacquaint her with his flavor. Memories of their single night together crowded her brain, and despite everything she tried to tell herself, she relaxed in his arms and let him have his way.

Whatever was on his mind, it seemed clear that he hadn't objected to taking her to his bed.

He threaded his fingers through her hair, holding her head at the exact angle he wanted, his other hand roaming over her back before finding its way under her shirt to play with her stiff nipples. She gasped into his mouth, her body readying itself for his possession, her panties growing damp as his kiss went on and on and on.

He lifted her onto the hood of his car, crowding her, wedging his hips between her thighs as he ravished her mouth and drove her arousal sky high. He rocked his hard cock against her aching pussy, her need for him overriding all sensible thought. She wanted him here, now. She'd dreamed of having him inside her again so many times that she wanted their clothes gone, to hell with the consequences.

"Perhaps we should take his little party inside," Alex said with a soft laugh in his voice.

Startled—how could she forget they had an audience?—Kali tried to pull out of Ronan's arms, but he held on tight, refusing even to let her wriggle.

"Be still," he ordered as he lifted away and looked into her eyes. She wasn't sure why, but she did as he asked and then just sat there on the hood of his car staring at him like some sort of pathetic, starry-eyed fan girl. "I wanted you that night," he said very clearly. He gripped her chin, forcing her to look at him even as she tried to look away. "I wanted you the morning you ran away." He pressed his cock harder against her crotch, smiling as she gasped from the pleasure. "And as you can see and feel, I very much want you now. Don't you dare doubt that."

"O–Okay," she managed to gasp out. Kali believed him. She wasn't sure exactly what that meant, but with mind-boggling arousal swirling through her she couldn't quite focus on anything else but the man in front of her.

Fortunately, Alex took care of that.

"Come on, beautiful," he said as he held out a hand for her to take. Confused, she glanced at Ronan, who stood back and let Alex help her off the car. Alex slung his arm over her shoulders and escorted her into the house, and she was shocked to find that she actually wanted to snuggle closer. Hell, she'd gone from begging Ronan for pity sex to a horny slut in less than five months. Alex was talking in a calm voice, but she had trouble taking in his words. Finally, after what were probably more than a few blank looks, Kali realized he was telling her about the precautions he'd installed inside this house. She took a deep, steadying breath and tried to focus.

The safe house was little more than a cabin in the middle of nowhere, but it did seem designed to act as a type of fortress. The only bedroom was in the center of the cabin and had a trapdoor leading to a type of panic room. She sure hoped they didn't need it, but it was kind of nice to know it was there.

Yet, despite what should have been time to calm down, she was still nearly vibrating with arousal as Alex led her into the kitchen where Ronan was making coffee.

* * * *

Alex couldn't quite tamp down the jealousy he felt. Male fire demons outnumbered female fire demons by about three to one, so he was quite used to sharing a woman, but his attraction had never been focused on a human female before. The worst part was that as the odd species out it was quite likely neither of them even realized he had feelings for Kali.

Come to think of it, he couldn't even explain why he had feelings for Kali. He'd only known the woman a handful of hours. He rubbed the headache forming behind his eyes and tried to get back to business.

"I spoke to your brother," he blurted out. Annoyed at his own uncharacteristic behavior, he dragged in a breath and forced a measure of calm into his voice. "He'd just been given the details of an attempted assassination. Apparently an officer arrived at the woman's home to warn her of the serial killer, heard her demanding that someone get the hell out of her house, and went in to offer assistance. The intruder, who looked to be a girl of about seven years of age, laughed and then seemed to disappear." He glanced at Kali. "I called in a favor from Brody, one of my squadmates, and he's going to watch over the woman until we can get her formal protection in one of our safe houses. The official police report says the girl ran from the scene, but I filled your brother in on what most likely happened. He wasn't as surprised as I was expecting." Alex shook his head and tried to get back on track. "Anyway, all four targets were born January twelfth between four fourteen and four twenty-two in the afternoon." He turned to Kali and couldn't resist running his knuckles down her soft cheek. "Unfortunately, beautiful, so were you." He glanced at

Ronan but couldn't gauge his friend's reaction to what was essentially him continuing to flirt with a woman who seemed important to the human.

"So they're going to protect the women who are targets?"

Alex nodded. "That's the plan. They're making a list now and hoping to pinpoint the potential targets. So far they've identified four, maybe five, more women." He smiled at her sigh of relief. "Statistically speaking, that's a rather high percentage, but apparently it's not unusual for a lot of human babies to be born the night of a full moon." Alex took a deep breath and reached out to touch Kali again before he could tell himself not to. "Your brother was quite accepting of the quick rundown I gave him on paranormal species and pixie assassins. I suspect he's seen enough in the past day or two to convince him there is more to the world than he knows." He winked at Kali and then turned his attention back to Ronan. "I spoke to my squad's acting CO, Thomas. He discussed it with our new administrative supervisor, and they've decided to follow standard protocols and involve the Ruling Body. That means our little secret is out." He reached over and grabbed Kali's hand. "It also means we'll have backup. Despite being on six months' leave, PUP Squad Alpha is being called back onto active duty. I explained Kali's situation to Thomas, and he's assigned me to her protection indefinitely."

Ronan looked relieved, but then he frowned as another problem apparently caught his attention. "You said earlier that pixies can follow your slip path." Alex nodded. "Do we have a way to lose them if they send more than one?"

Alex grinned. Ronan was always thinking, always planning. It was why his business was so well known in the paranormal community.

"I spoke to Jason—he's a warlock with my PUP squad," he said for Kali's benefit. Ronan had worked with most of the members of PUP Squad Alpha one time or another over the past decade. "Jason will transport us if it becomes necessary. Pixies can't follow a warlock's bounce tunnel, so all we have to do is get to him via slip travel and we'll lose any pixie pursuers easily enough."

"How will you find Jason?" Kali asked, looking intrigued rather than frightened.

"Sorry, beautiful, I should have explained that. Jason is the only member of PUP Squad Alpha to remain on leave. He's dealing with a family issue, so all we have to do is slip travel to his home."

Now Kali looked concerned, and if Alex had to guess he'd say it was because she didn't want to intrude on the warlock's private life.

"Don't worry," Ronan said to her, apparently sensing the same thing as Alex. "We'll only go to him as a last resort."

"Okay," she said looking relieved.

Ronan wrapped his arm around Kali's shoulder, holding her close as he waited for Alex to give him a report on the rest.

"Thomas is also talking to the Ruling Body right now, but at the moment their orders are to protect the potential targets in tandem with human law enforcement without revealing who we are. I'm not sure how effective my squadmates will be working alongside random police officers, so it might be an idea to call in your team."

"Your team?" Kali asked Ronan with a quirked eyebrow.

Ronan didn't look like he was going to answer, so Alex answered for him. "Ronan is the head of Deeks Security. They offer discreet, secure protection for some of the highest-profile people in the world—human *and* paranormal."

"Oh," Kali said, looking surprised. "My brother didn't tell me any of that. I thought you were just an old army buddy."

Ronan smiled then. "I *am* an old army buddy of Dave's. I started the company around the same time he joined the police force." He grinned as if remembering back to those days. "I actually offered him a job, but he chose to get married instead. Apparently he'd had enough of traveling the world."

"But he didn't know about paranormals until today?"

"Nope. Obviously if he'd come to work for me, I would have filled him in, but Dave seemed to want to put the whole army experience behind him. I was actually a little surprised that he joined the police force, but he seems to like it."

"When he's not tracking down pixie assassins," Kali said with a frown as she stepped away from Ronan's embrace. She still looked a little disturbed by her introduction to the world of paranormal species, but she was handling it better than most humans he'd known. Alex wanted to pull her into his arms—his attraction to this woman confusing and damn near overwhelming—but moved away instead. He glanced at the clock even though he knew perfectly well what time it was.

"The sun will go down in a couple of hours. I've got the wards in place and the perimeter alarm set, so we should get ample warning of any visitors. I think I'll go catch some sleep while I have the chance."

"Sure," Ronan said in a neutral tone. "I'll sort out something for dinner."

"Sweet," Alex said with a quick nod and tried to leave the room without looking like he was escaping. Judging by the next question Kali asked, he hadn't been successful.

* * * *

"Is he okay?" Kali whispered to Ronan as Alex seemed to flee the room.

"He can hear you," Ronan said in a normal voice, "and no, he's probably not okay."

"Why?" He could hear the concern in her voice and fell for her just a little bit harder. Everything he'd noticed about her that first night was simply being confirmed in every word, every smile, every touch.

"Fire demons are different to humans." She quirked an eyebrow and waited for a better explanation. "What I mean is fire demons share their mates with at least two other males, usually three or four."

"I don't understand why that would upset him. I'm not a prude or anything. I'm not going to judge a species for their mating habits." She was so adorable when she was confused, but since he was usually the one to put his foot in his mouth when it came to women, he probably wasn't the best person to explain. Ironically, despite the jealousy he'd felt earlier, he wasn't upset that Alex liked Kali. She was an amazing person. What wasn't there to like?

"Why don't you go get some rest? I'll call you for dinner."

"I…um…there's only one bed."

"That's okay. I'm sure Alex won't mind."

"What about you? Will you mind?"

"Not at all," he said with a grin. But when her smile disappeared, he realized she'd taken that the wrong way. Hell, maybe he'd spent too much time around paranormals. Most humans would find the idea of two men with one woman rather strange. "Kali," he said, trying to choose his words carefully. "Alex is as attracted to you as I am. If you want to explore that, it's fine. I'm happy for you."

"B–But I thought you liked me." Tears filled her eyes, and he gathered her into his arms quickly.

"I do like you," he assured her, running his fingers through her thick curls, mentally kicking himself. "Alex, get out here. I'm fucking this up."

* * * *

Kali wanted to cry. Granted, it had been a very strange day, but Ronan's rejection really stung. When they'd been kissing on the hood of the car, she'd found a peace that had eluded her for months. How stupid was that? They'd been making out like a couple of horny teenagers, and she'd felt happy. Shit, she'd promised him she wouldn't throw herself at him again, yet here she was. Talk about pathetic, but he'd seemed so sincere in his words at the time. Had something gone wrong between them since then?

"I always said you were a jackass when it came to women," Alex said to Ronan as he pulled Kali from his arms and settled her on a stool near the bench. "What my verbally challenged friend is trying to say is that he's loved you since he met you."

Kali shook her head. That seemed an erroneous assumption. Technically she and Ronan had known each other for less than twenty-four hours. The sex had been amazing, incredible even, and she'd been more attracted to him than any man she'd ever known— she glanced at Alex and amended that to *almost* any man she'd ever known—but using the word "love" seemed a huge exaggeration.

"No buts, beautiful. I've never seen him react to a woman the way he reacts to you." He leaned in and added in a conspiratorial whisper, "He probably doesn't remember telling me about you, but he was pretty torn up when you ran the way you did."

"So why did he suggest I go sleep with you?"

"I'm pretty sure he meant sleep *beside* me…for now at least." She could feel heated embarrassment creeping over her face—she hadn't meant to make assumptions—but then he confused her even more by adding, "I'm sure between the two of us we can make you happy."

"So that thing about sharing a mate, that's what you two want to do?"

"It's probably too early to be making any decisions like that," Alex said after a quick glance at Ronan. "All we ask is that you keep an open mind. Just know that if you want both of us, it isn't a problem. And well, if you decide to go all human on us and choose only one, well we can deal with that, too."

Kali could almost see the pain behind that statement. She felt certain that Alex had been hurt that way before. She knew it in her heart. She had no way of explaining, even to herself, the sureness of what she was sensing, but she felt very confident that what she "knew" was right. But blurting it out seemed inappropriate at this moment. She wanted to lighten the mood, say something or do something that would give them all a chance to breathe, but the words wouldn't come.

She smiled when Ronan stepped closer, pressed his lips to hers for a moment, and then placed her hand over his erection. "Go get some rest. Whatever happens between you two, just know that I still want you just as much as I did five months ago."

She nodded, biting her bottom lip to keep her tears from spilling. Ronan may seem a gruff soldier, but he truly cared for people, and despite the fact that they were different species, he thought of Alex as a brother. How she knew that, again, she had no idea, but the feeling that she was correct stayed with her even as she fell asleep cuddled in Alex's arms.

Chapter Five

"What's for breakfast?"

Ronan glanced over at Alex and tried not to growl. Four days without an attack should have made him happy, but boredom was setting in for all of them. There were only so many card games three adults could play before they were climbing up the walls—figuratively speaking of course.

"Eggs," Ronan answered, not caring to elaborate. He'd discovered after an inedible dinner and two burned breakfasts that both of his roommates were lousy cooks. If he wanted to enjoy eating, he had to do the cooking himself.

He cracked several eggs into a bowl and was adding salt and pepper as Kali wandered into the kitchen. She looked adorable in his rumpled shirt, and he already had half a hard-on just looking at her. His cock drew to full salute when she wrapped her arms around Alex's waist and accepted his passionate good-morning kiss. A moment later, she moved into Ronan's arms and he did the same, practically inhaling her with his need to stamp her with his possession. She'd slept between both men each night, but so far nothing more than some rather zealous kissing had gone on between them.

Ronan tried desperately to think of something else—at least until he had breakfast cooked.

"Did Dave have any news?" Kali asked.

"Not today," he answered with a slow shake of his head.

He ran into the nearest town each morning to call Dave from the payphone, but so far the only news he'd had was that they'd been able to track down only one of the five other women born around the same time as Kali. The woman—the same one who'd been attacked and had survived by sheer lucky timing—was currently being protected by one of Ronan's employees, Nathan, working with one of Alex's squadmates, a shifter called Brody. As a precaution they'd all abandoned technology, and so his only contact with any of them was through Dave.

"I wonder where they are," Kali mused out loud for about the hundredth time. The other four women's whereabouts remained a mystery. It was quite possible that they were already dead, but Ronan drew hope from the fact that if neither his team nor Alex's PUP squad could find them, there was a good chance the assassins couldn't either.

Alex also had one of his brothers and several others in the paranormal community unofficially investigating the Oracle's murder. The fact that twenty-seven years had passed was making it very difficult, but with a bit of luck they might be able to identify who killed her and why. From there they should be able to neutralize whoever the threat was coming from now.

But, while all that was going on, they had no choice but to sit tight and wait for someone else to make a breakthrough. Sitting idle while others did the investigative work wasn't his usual habit, but this time he wasn't willing to hand over protection duty to anyone. Kali was too important—to him and to Alex.

They talked idly about the case through breakfast, but since they had no new information they were really only rehashing the same stuff over and over.

"Can we talk about us?" Kali asked, changing the topic unexpectedly. Ronan glanced up to see Alex wore the same surprised expression he could feel on his own face.

"Sure, beautiful. What's on your mind?" Kali looked a little disconcerted by Alex's flippant-seeming attitude, and Ronan wanted to kick him under the table. Wasn't Alex supposed to be the one who was good at this stuff?

"I don't know how to explain it," Kali said, coloring a little with embarrassment, "but I feel a connection to you both."

Ronan reached over and grabbed her hand. "It's okay, Kali. We already discussed this. Do what you feel is right for you. If you want both of us, or only one, or neither, it's not going to affect our friendship or how we protect you."

She smiled and squeezed his hand then took a deep breath, seeming to search for the right words. "You see...the thing is...I know stuff about you that you haven't told me." She shook her head in a wobbly sort of way, rolled her eyes, and tried again. "I *think* I know stuff about you. Both of you. I don't know how to explain it. It's kind of like having memories that aren't actually mine." She turned her gaze to Alex and held out her other hand for him to take. "Somehow I know you've been hurt before. I even think that it was your brothers' partner who hurt you. She chose the other three but not you." She shook her head and closed her eyes. "Shit. I'm probably insane. I mean, I keep thinking I know things, but how can I know things? It doesn't make any sense."

Judging by Alex's complete stillness, Ronan was beginning to wonder just how close Kali's assessment was. He'd suspected for a long time that Alex's womanizing and charming ways were a reaction to something that had broken him long ago, but he'd never suspected that it might have been his sister-in-law who'd done the breaking. Yet it would explain the strained relationship he had with his brothers. They always invited Alex to family events. Alex always found an excuse not to attend.

Kali watched Alex for a moment before releasing a deep breath and turning back to Ronan. "No sense in making a fool of myself only partway." She gave him a lopsided smile. "I keep thinking that you've never had a connection—with anyone. You hold yourself away from everyone, even your army buddies." She lowered her eyes and whispered the rest. "The only true connection you've felt was with me." She shook her head as if to clear it. "But there's something else there. A need to have Alex included, almost like he is a necessary part of this...of us."

She dropped her head forward, but not before Ronan saw the tears leak past her closed eyelids.

"Kali," he said as he tried to gather the woman in his arms. But she resisted, pulling away with a half laugh, half sob.

"That's...um...probably wishful thinking on my part. Shit! I'm nuts *and* pathetic." She started backing away. "Sorry."

Alex caught her as she tried to leave the room, pulling her into his arms and then moving to trap her between them.

"You're not nuts," Alex said in a voice more serious than Ronan had ever heard the fire demon use. "Stephanie mated two of my brothers when I was quite young—well, young in demon terms. I did love her for many years, but she has only ever seen me as a younger brother, never as a potential mate. It didn't really hurt until she chose my youngest brother as well a few years later."

"I was right?" Kali asked, sounding rather shocked.

"Yes," Alex said as he pressed a kiss to her lips, gently deepening the contact when she opened her mouth for him. Ronan could feel his cock swelling just watching his friend kiss his woman. And she was his woman. He had absolutely no doubt about that.

He smoothed his hands around her waist and undid the buttons of her shirt with clumsy fingers. She moaned when he caressed her stiff nipples, pushing the material aside, exposing her to Alex's touch. Alex groaned when Kali lifted his hands to her breasts, pressing his fingers against her soft flesh without breaking their kiss.

Ronan went to move away, happy to step back as Kali and Alex got to know each other, but Kali made a soft sound of disappointment, and he couldn't do it. He'd often envied fire demons for their mating habits, and now more than ever he understood why. There was just something magical about sharing a woman he cared deeply for with a man who cared for her also.

Smoothing the shirt off her shoulders, Ronan pressed kisses to the back of her neck as Alex lowered to his knees and worshipped her breasts. She was completely naked without the shirt. They'd had to leave her home so quickly she only had Ronan's and Alex's clothes to wear while they were here. Ronan knew he should have picked up some things for her in town, but he'd used the excuse that buying clothes for a female might give away her hiding place. It had been an extreme precaution, and if he'd truly been honest, he would have admitted it was more likely an excuse because he enjoyed seeing her in his shirts. Fortunately, he didn't make a habit of looking at his motivations too closely.

He groaned as Kali caressed his cock through his jeans, the soft touch both new and achingly familiar. Desperately, he helped her to undo the buttons, and then she wrapped her warm fingers around his hard erection. He groaned and thanked whatever deity had urged him to go commando today. He snaked a hand around her hip, caressing the crease at the top of her leg as Alex moved lower, licking a path down to the pussy Ronan had been dreaming about for months.

Ronan knew the exact moment Alex's tongue found her clit because she gasped and her balance wobbled. He leaned back against the bench, lifted her off her feet, and spread her wide for Alex's sweet torture. Her head fell back onto Ronan's chest, her eyes unfocused as she looked up at him and then back down at what Alex was doing.

At this angle Ronan could see Alex flicking his tongue over her clit. She writhed in their combined grasp, her orgasm approaching at light speed. Alex moved lower, thrusting his tongue deep into her pussy as his fingers found her clit. She shook all over, her breathing barely gasps as Alex expertly held her at the precipice, giving her only enough to keep her there.

But then he moved away slightly, nodded to Ronan, and stood up to press his mouth against Kali's. Kali wriggled in Ronan's arms, trying to press back against his hard cock. It took a moment for the meaning of their actions to sink in, but Ronan finally realized what they both wanted him to do.

He lifted Kali higher, fitting his hard cock against her entrance. All three of them groaned as Kali sank onto his erection, her pussy surrounding him in heavenly warmth.

Alex broke his kiss with Kali to look at her face. "I think she likes that," he said with a knowing grin. Kali nodded enthusiastically, wrapping one arm behind her to hold Ronan to her and one arm around Alex to draw him back. He went with a smile on his face, his obvious contentment a reflection of Ronan's own. "You look so beautiful like this, Kali."

Ronan felt her pussy clench in reaction to that statement. He smiled at Alex and then held Kali tighter as he started pumping into her body, fucking her slowly, savoring the moment. But Alex must have had his fingers on her clit because Kali started to wriggle, seeming uncertain whether she wanted to move toward Alex or shimmy away. But Ronan took the choice from her, thrusting harder into her, pushing her against Alex's hand with increasing speed.

Kali released a keening cry and then exploded into orgasm, her entire body shaking as she moaned her delight. Her pussy muscles caressed his cock, the delicious sensations dragging him with her, his climax bursting from him as Alex did something that forced Kali into orgasm once more.

Ronan leaned harder against the bench, holding Kali tight as she finally stilled in his arms. She rested against him, and he held her closer, trying to catch his breath. After a few moments Ronan slid his cock from her pussy and Alex moved forward, kissing Kali hard, thrusting his tongue into her mouth over and over as if to mimic what he wanted.

Kali lifted her legs higher, wrapping them around Alex's hips, pulling him closer, even as Ronan held her up. Ronan felt Alex's almost violent entry reverberate through Kali's entire body. She groaned, one hand still wrapped behind her to hold Ronan close, the other curled around Alex's neck as he kissed her, ravaging her mouth, stamping his possession on her as thoroughly as Ronan had moments ago.

She lifted into every thrust, claiming Alex, taking her fill as she shook with impending orgasm once more. But this time Alex didn't tease. This time he threw them both over the edge, fucking her harder, groaning when she shook violently and moaned her climax. He ground against her, the action pushing her more firmly against Ronan, his shock at sharing both of their orgasms overridden only by the wonder of feeling somehow complete.

He held Kali close, loving her more each moment as she tiredly caressed both men. Alex eventually pulled out of her pussy and kissed her gently before moving away. He righted his clothing and then helped Kali to stand so that Ronan could do the same. Hell, neither of them had even gotten undressed. They'd just taken her like wild things, fucking her without finesse, without regard to her comfort or needs.

The apology barely made it out of his mouth before Kali turned to him, annoyance crossing her face a moment before she smiled and leaned over to touch his cheek. "None of that," she said quietly. "I enjoyed every moment." And then her grin turned impish and her gaze bounced between him and Alex. "And I do find a certain pride in being able to incite such need in both of you that you didn't even have time to take your clothes off."

Alex laughed, wrapped his arms around her from behind, and looked at Ronan with a smile. "Is it any wonder we love the woman?" he asked with a soft laugh.

* * * *

Love.

Only a few days ago Kali would have denied that such a deep emotion could grow so quickly, but now she wondered if it were possible. Both men seemed to care for her, and even though she knew Alex's words weren't meant as a declaration, she couldn't quite squash the hope that someday it might be true.

"Why don't you go have a shower, beautiful," Alex said with a wink. "I'll meet you in bed in a few minutes."

She smiled, already suspecting that he wanted a few moments with Ronan to make sure he was okay with all of this. Even though it had essentially been Ronan's idea, it seemed Alex didn't want to risk their relationship with any misunderstandings.

Kali stepped into the shower, sighing as the hot water caressed her skin. She tried really hard not to dream of all the things she wanted in her future. It didn't work.

* * * *

Ronan eyed his friend warily. He and Alex had known each other for a long time, yet right at this moment he had no idea what the fire demon was thinking.

"Are you going to be all right with this?"

"Of course," Ronan said, feeling a little bit confused.

"So I don't need to disable the weapons you own that could hurt me," Alex said with his usual grin.

"No," Ronan said with a quick laugh. "Well, not unless you plan on hurting Kali. Then you might want to run."

"I have no plans to hurt her, but you already know that." Alex tilted his head slightly to the side and looked at Ronan as if he were considering whether to say something else or not.

"Spit it out, Alex. You've known me long enough to know I don't need sugar coating."

"I was just wondering if you realize you're the only human in this relationship." Ronan ground his teeth together and nodded. He wasn't sure Kali even realized she could do it, but seeing her coffee cup move by itself to slide into her hand several times over the last couple days certainly seemed to be a skill typical to some paranormals. He wasn't aware of any humans who actually had telekinetic abilities. There were a lot of con artists and illusionists, but none had proven genuine telekinetic ability.

"You think she's the Oracle's receptacle?" Ronan asked quietly.

"Not really," Alex answered slowly, managing to confuse Ronan even more. "The Oracles only possess knowledge. I'm not sure where Kali's skill is coming from." He glanced at the bathroom door and lowered his voice even more. "But it certainly isn't a skill I would associate with a full-blood human."

"Are you saying paranormals and humans can interbreed?"

"Some species, yes."

"Fire demons?"

"Not sure," Alex answered with a shrug. "I don't know any other fire demons who've taken a human as their mate."

It was finally beginning to dawn on Ronan that they hadn't used condoms. Could Kali be conceiving a child even now? Unexpectedly, the thought filled him with a type of joy, an excitement he couldn't quite explain, rather than the dread he would have felt had it been someone else.

He glanced up to see Kali watching them from the bedroom door.

"Kali," he said with grim determination to 'fess up, "I'm sorry, baby."

"What for?" she asked, looking really worried. He felt like a complete jackass. They were supposed to be protecting her, and instead he'd managed to put her at risk of an unplanned pregnancy.

"We didn't use contraception," Alex said, looking as concerned by Kali's reaction as Ronan felt.

Kali smiled with obvious relief. "It's okay. I have an IUD, so you don't need to worry about babies or—what do you call baby demons?" She shook her head and continued without waiting for an answer. "I...was actually...um..." She took a deep breath and frowned at them both. "You don't think I'm human?"

"We don't know anything for sure, but the fact that you can move things using telekinesis would suggest something is different."

"I can do what?"

Alex smiled, lifted a coffee cup from the sink, and placed it in the middle of the table. "Just reach for the cup."

Kali looked skeptical, but she leaned over to grab the cup, jumping back in surprise when it slid toward her hand.

"I don't understand," she said, shaking her head, obviously not believing her own eyes. She closed them for a moment, rubbed her forehead, and whispered, "I'm pretty sure I've never been able to do that before. Shit! You know how I said before that I just sort of know things. I feel like I should know where this skill comes from, but…" She made that funny face again that Ronan was beginning to realize was her version of frustration. "It's kind of like having a book with no index. I think the information is in there. I just can't find it."

"So you are the Oracle's receptacle?" Alex asked, looking confused.

Kali shrugged. "From everything you've told me about the Oracles, I would have to say no. But then it doesn't explain what's happening to me, and it sure as hell doesn't explain why it's happening now."

"Does anyone else in your family have unusual skills?" Alex asked. "Any psychics, or ghost hunters, or other kooky ancestors? Maybe one of them was a paranormal."

"I had a great-uncle nobody talked about, but I don't really know why."

"Would your brother know?"

She shrugged. "Probably not."

Ronan smiled at the way Alex moved to hold her. They seemed so natural together. He probably should have felt some sort of jealousy, but he only felt honored to know he was a part of their happiness. He didn't feel left out. For the first time in a long time he felt part of a family. Kali saw his smile, blew him a soft kiss, and winked slowly.

Ronan couldn't help but grin even wider. Only a handful of days ago he would have been appalled by the sappy emotions coursing through him, but right now all he could do was smile.

But of course, their unusual relationship wasn't going to go anywhere if they didn't figure out who was trying to kill Kali and find a way to stop them.

"I'm going to drive into town and call Dave again. He might be able to dig up some family skeletons and answer a question or two."

"Get him to contact one of my brothers," Alex added. "My family should be able to make some discreet inquiries from the paranormal side. If you do have a nonhuman relative, they might have more chance to track them down. I doubt human records would keep information like that."

Ronan nodded, grabbed his keys and some coins for the phone, and pressed a quick kiss to Kali's lips. "Don't have too much fun without me," he said with a wink and then turned and left the cabin quickly. As much as he hated leaving her behind, he was suddenly impatient to get some answers so that they could get on with the rest of their lives.

* * * *

As Alex locked the door and reset the alarm, he realized that at least part of Ronan's reason for going in to town was to give him and Kali some time alone together. "Do you think he's okay?" he asked Kali.

"I think so," she answered with a smile.

"So this 'knowing things' skill," he said with a wicked grin as he pulled her back into his embrace and ran a hand over her hip, caressing her through the damp towel. "Can you tell what I'm thinking now?"

She laughed, the lyrical sound filling the room. "Well…my skill doesn't seem to be mindreading as such, but I'm guessing that your thinking has something to do with sex."

"You can feel my horniness?"

Kali pressed a kiss to his lips and then snuggled deeper into his arms. "Well, I doubt it's a paranormal skill," she said with an almost laugh, "but the hard cock pressed against my stomach gave me a pretty *solid* clue."

He mock growled and ran his hands all over her ass, slipping the material aside so that he could squeeze and caress her soft flesh. He slid one of his hands around to her front, wedging it between them, his finger delving into her folds, sliding along her slippery flesh before pushing up inside of her pussy.

"I think maybe I'm developing some 'knowing' skills of my own," he said with what he hoped was the right amount of humor, "because I do believe you're feeling the same things."

She giggled, stepped from his arms, and gave him a very serious look. His heart nearly stopped beating when she dropped the towel to the ground. "Do you think," she said, biting her lip in a blatantly sexual tease, "that if I ran into the bedroom, you might follow?"

"I might actually beat you there," he said with a wide grin.

"Good to know," she said calmly. And then, with a gleeful laugh her only warning, she turned and ran.

Chapter Six

Kali ran into the bedroom, giggling as she almost made it to the bed before Alex caught up with her. His momentum took them down onto the mattress, but it was the way he tickled her that had her writhing with uncontrollable laughter.

"Uncle, uncle, uncle, uncle," she managed to force out between giggles.

"Hmm," he said, pretending to consider her plea. "This must be some of that human code that we demons have not yet been able to decipher." It was quite obvious that he was teasing, but when his tickles turned to sensual strokes, Kali could barely breathe for a whole different reason.

"Do you think," she asked breathlessly, "that you might have enough warning to take your clothes off this time?"

He laughed, kissing her ear before sucking the lobe into his mouth and tickling the flesh with his tongue. "It could be a possibility." He slid down the mattress, sucking her neck as his clever fingers found her taut nipples and squeezed gently. "Although, if you keep moaning like that it might be touch and go."

She giggled again, amazed to realize just how much fun she was having with him. Alex groaned, rolled off the bed, and onto his feet in one fluid movement. He dragged his clothes off, but she noticed that he pulled a small remote control from his pants pocket and kept it in his palm.

"What's that?" she asked curiously.

"The remote to turn off the wards." When she gave him a curious look, he added, "You might prefer to call them a type of force field.

They basically stop any supernatural creature from entering the building via slip travel. Trouble is that it also keeps us in. If we need to slip quickly, I can hit the remote, turn off the wards, and transport you and Ronan, if I can reach him, to somewhere safe."

"You'd leave Ronan behind?" The irony to her question was that she could feel Alex's determination to keep them both safe but got the impression that Ronan didn't really need his protection.

"Trust me. The big guy is one of the most feared humans in the paranormal world."

"Seriously?" How weird was it that she somehow knew he was telling the truth but expressed disbelief anyway? It seemed *knowing* stuff didn't stop her from *saying* stupid stuff.

But then Alex moved back onto the bed and Kali was suddenly completely distracted by the fact that the man was naked. He truly was a delicious specimen. Handsome features, sculpted muscles, hard in all the right places. Kali reached for the hard part that interested her the most, and he moaned even as he tried to inch away.

"I'm not sure that's such a good decision, beautiful."

"Why not?" she asked with an impish smile as she slid lower on the bed and pressed her mouth to the head of his cock.

"I...I have no idea," he said with a dramatic sigh. She laughed again, enjoying the playfulness of her demon lover. But he gave up all pretense of humor when she slid her mouth lower, swirling her tongue around the head of his cock before suctioning her lips around him and sucking hard. He groaned and threaded his fingers through her hair, massaging her scalp as he lifted up to thrust gently into her mouth. She wrapped her fist around the base of his cock, pumping and squeezing as she sucked harder.

But then his fingers tightened in her hair, pulling her away from his erection. She broke the suction reluctantly but moaned in appreciation when he climbed over her, threaded his hands under her knees, and drove his cock into her hard and fast.

Alex plunged into her pussy several times, thrusting forward quickly, pulling away slowly. He slid his hands up her legs, cupping her ass, angling her to the position he wanted. Kali could feel her orgasm spinning closer, her need for this man breathtaking.

But then he froze.

The sound of the front door opening sent terror pounding through her until they heard Ronan's deep voice. Alex fell forward and pressed a kiss to her lips, his body thrusting into hers over and over as Ronan came into the bedroom.

"Roll over," Ronan said on a low growl. She didn't even think of denying him. Alex held her close as he rolled onto his back, taking her with him so that she lay sprawled over his body. "Now that is a pretty sight." Ronan's hands caressed her ass, his fingers dipping between her crease as Alex continued to thrust up into her pussy. "Have you ever had a man in your ass?"

"N–No," she whispered. A wicked thrill wound through her as Alex grabbed her knees, pulling her legs higher up his body, opening her ass cheeks to Ronan's touch even more.

"Tell me you bought lube," Alex demanded as he plowed harder into her pussy.

Ronan chuckled quietly. "I bought lube." He caressed her spine, his warm hands a soothing counterpoint to Alex's hard thrusts. "But it's Kali's choice. Will you let us take you together?"

"Together?" she managed to ask even though her climax was so close she felt like she could fly into a million pieces at any moment.

"Me in your pussy. Ronan in your ass," Alex whispered. "Just imagine, you'll be stuffed full of cock, so overwhelmed with pleasure that you won't know where you end and we begin."

She nodded, gasping for air as they wound their sensual promises through her mind. "Yes," she said by way of a plea. She wanted this with them, wanted the closeness, the feeling of being complete, of being one with both of her men.

Alex stilled, holding her pressed hard against him as he kissed her ferociously. She whimpered into his mouth as she heard the squirt of lube a moment before Ronan's slippery finger pressed against her virgin hole. "Easy, baby," Ronan crooned as he circled the tight ring of muscle without pushing inside. "We'll take this slowly."

She made a noise that she hoped sounded like agreement and then moaned into Alex's mouth as he threaded his fingers through her hair and deepened their kiss. She felt his cock pulse inside her, Ronan's finger slowly pressing into her ass making the fit seem tighter.

The second finger stung more than she expected, and she squirmed away from Ronan's touch. But he pressed a hand against her lower spine, trapping her against Alex. "It's okay, baby," he said as he added more lube and gently opened her tight muscles. "Relax."

Uh-huh. Relaxing didn't seem to be part of her makeup at the moment. Even now with the sting in her ass almost unbearable she was on the verge of orgasm. She shifted, trying to do as Ronan ordered but only managing to make Alex groan with her.

Alex broke their kiss and grabbed her hips, lifting her high enough to pull his cock from her pussy. She whimpered at the loss but groaned as he found her clit with his fingers and rubbed the hard nub gently.

"That's it, baby," Ronan said as he added yet another finger to her ass. She started to push back against him, the strange sensation no longer painful but enticingly erotic. She heard him squirt more lube a moment before the head of his cock replaced his fingers. The spongy, slippery head of his dick felt completely different, and she moaned as it stretched her even wider.

He slid unhurriedly into her back passage, his movement gentle, undemanding as she gradually adjusted to his possession. He pulled from her ass slowly before sliding back in, thrusting just a little harder, just a little faster, just a little more urgently with each stroke. She gasped, the unexpected pleasure burning through her as Ronan took her to heights of arousal she'd never thought possible.

Alex continued to play with her clit even when Ronan lifted her up so that Alex could slide back into her pussy. The fit was tight, the sensation overwhelming as they worked together, building a rhythm, one thrusting in as the other slid out. Over and over they fucked her.

And then, just as she started to shake all over, her orgasm winding tighter, spiraling higher, leaving her breathless, out of her mind, balancing on the edge of desire, a loud shrieking noise filled the air. Climax slammed her, the world tilting off its axis, her body vibrating as her release pounded through her.

* * * *

Alex heard the perimeter alarm just as his cum burst from him, bathing the inside of Kali's body with his seed. Groaning both with his release and the urgent need to concentrate, Alex flicked the remote control, placed a hand on Ronan's shoulder, and transported them nearly a mile into the forest behind the house.

He kissed Kali, silencing her frantic scream as her pussy milked his cock of every last drop. Ronan groaned above them, his orgasm obviously triggered by Kali's own.

And then Alex rolled them over, pushing Kali into Ronan's arms as he pulled from her heavenly warmth and waited for whoever had attacked them to follow his slip path. The pixie didn't disappoint, appearing a moment later only a few feet away. Obviously intent on getting close enough to hurt Kali, the pixie managed to dodge his fire attack. However, the assassin didn't count on Ronan's response and burst into flame the moment the bullet filled with demon shot hit her stomach. Alex smiled at his friend's obvious ability to grab his gun even though all three of them had been preoccupied at the time.

"The spray glue under the bed," Ronan said breathlessly as he managed to somehow pull Kali behind him and aim the gun at the pixie's collapsing ash pile. Alex nodded, slipped back to the house, located the aerosol can, and slipped back to the forest. Ronan was already kicking the ashes apart. A few sprays of sticky glue held them apart. Each time that there was any movement from the ashes, either paranormal or from the wind, Ronan sprayed some more. Alex smiled at his friend's ingenuity. Pixies were simply considered unstoppable amongst the paranormal community, so nobody had ever given any real thought as to how one might slow their reformation down. As Ronan obviously expected, the pixie didn't rematerialize.

"Shit! That is not what I expected when we climbed into bed," Kali said with a strange sort of smile on her face as she picked herself up off the ground. She peeked at the mess of glue and ash from a safe distance. "Is she dead for real this time?"

"Not sure," Alex said with a smile of his own. "Nobody has ever thought to glue pixie ashes down." He turned to Ronan, adrenaline and relief playing havoc with his own emotions. "Always knew you were handy to have around in a fight."

Ronan dipped his head in acknowledgement but seemed to be all business. "How far are we from the house?"

"Only about a mile or so."

"Okay, slip back to the house, grab us some clothes, and we'll walk back."

"Hey," Alex said as he realized that neither Ronan nor Kali seemed as nauseated as they had last time they'd traveled by slip. "You're both okay?"

Ronan pulled Kali into his arms and pressed a kiss to the top of her head. "I'm fine. How about you, baby?"

"I…um…seem to be pretty good." She screwed up her face a moment and added, "Except for the fact that I'm standing naked in the middle of a forest and really need a shower." She made a face as she tried to brush leaves, dirt, and other forest debris from her beautifully curved body

"I could just—" Alex began to offer, but Ronan held up a hand to stop him.

"I suspect that the reason we're fine is due to the fact that we were both in the middle of orgasm at the time. Our senses were otherwise engaged. So, thanks for the offer, but I'd rather walk."

"No problems," Alex said as he turned to Kali and winked. "That's something I'll remember for next time though."

* * * *

"Do I have time for a shower?" Kali asked as they finally made it back into the house. The moment Ronan nodded she stripped the shirt straight off and headed for the bathroom. "Will she come after me again?"

"We have no way of knowing," Ronan said as he stepped into the shower behind her. "But I'm guessing that even if a pixie can reform after being incinerated and glued, it will take her some time. I doubt they'll send a replacement assassin just yet."

"That's true," Alex said from the doorway, "and since nobody officially knows how to kill a pixie, it's likely they'll just assume she's still working on it."

"So you think she's dead?" Kali asked quietly. It didn't really sit well with her, but if the choice were her or the pixie, she was very glad to be the one still standing.

Alex just shrugged.

"How do pixies normally die? Do they grow old?" Ronan asked as he finished cleaning himself down and turned his attention to her. His warm hands were rather distracting despite the impersonal efficiency he was using.

"I doubt anyone but the pixies know about pixies," Alex said. "There's a lot of folklore surrounding them, even in the paranormal communities, but I don't know what's true and what's not."

"So we really need to get out of here in case she can overcome the glue and reform?"

"Yes," Ronan said as he dragged Kali out from under the water and wrapped a towel around her. Alex stepped under the water and washed quickly.

He was just drying himself off when the perimeter alarm sounded again.

Chapter Seven

Ronan already had his gun in his hand. He shook his head as Alex looked ready to slip travel them to another destination. It would give them a few moments before the pixie could follow, but their position was probably more defensible here than anywhere else. With the wards reengaged the pixie wouldn't be able to slip travel away from them. Obviously the spray glue hadn't worked. Maybe if they gathered the dust in several airtight, glue-filled jars she wouldn't be able to re-form. He'd try that next time.

They held their ground, the bathroom almost as defensible as the bedroom. It had only one small window not even large enough for a child, or pixie of childlike size, to climb through. That left only the single doorway, and with Ronan and Alex both armed and ready their attacker had little chance of getting past.

The minutes dragged on, the screech of the alarm getting more and more annoying by the moment. Just when Ronan was beginning to wonder if the pixie planned to wait them out, something flew toward them. At first it seemed to be a very big dragonfly, but as it drew nearer Ronan recognized its petite features.

"Is that what I think it is?" Kali asked as she peeked out from behind Alex.

"I guess that explains what happens to a pixie who gets most of her ashes glued together," Alex said with what was obviously meant to be a mocking laugh. Despite her size, Ronan wasn't willing to relax his guard, and he was quite grateful to his friend for trying to fire up their enemy's temper. Chances were if the pixie got angry, she would do something poorly thought through.

Fortunately, Alex's instincts proved correct a moment later as the irate, miniature pixie made a strange sort of hissing noise and went for Ronan's face. He managed to grab her in the palm of his hand, but the little bitch burned him a couple of times before he could get her into a jar in the kitchen. Fortunately, her size meant the burns were no worse than the touch of a lit cigarette—annoying but ultimately not fatal.

She carried on for a while, hissing as loudly as she could—which wasn't really all that loud—and beating her fragile-looking wings against the confined space of the jar. Surprisingly she cringed away in fear when Ronan grabbed a nail and hammer but seemed to calm down when she realized he only intended to punch a couple of holes in the lid so she could get some air.

"Too bad she doesn't glow in the dark," Alex said with a smirk. "She'd make a rather pretty lantern." The pixie gave him a nasty look and used her finger in a way Ronan thought was typical only of humans. "I'm assuming that she can still slip travel, so the jar will only hold her while the wards are in place." The pixie looked rather interested until he added, "And since I have no intention of turning them off, we should be able to hold her indefinitely." She slumped to the bottom of the jar. It was obvious that she was saying something, but between her size and the glass Ronan wasn't able to hear her.

"Were you able to catch any of that?" Ronan asked Alex.

"Not a word," Alex said, smirking when their captive flipped him the bird once more.

"I'd really like to know why she still came after us. If that's as big as she's going to get, it put her at a tactical disadvantage. A human assassin would have cancelled the job or maybe called in help."

"Didn't I see karaoke equipment in the television cabinet?" Kali asked. "Maybe we can rig up one of the microphones to the TV."

Ronan shuddered at the thought that he'd spent time in a house that was harboring such equipment. Thank God nobody had asked him to sing. There was a limit to how much one man should be asked to sacrifice in the name of keeping his woman safe and happy.

They had the microphone set up a few minutes later, and of course that was when the annoying little assassin decided to shut up. Angry enough to shake the jar, but sensible enough not to, Ronan turned to Alex for help. Nothing he'd learned about interrogation techniques had included a course on how to make a three-inch pixie spill all.

* * * *

"Why did you come after me?" Kali asked their captive.

The pixie rolled her eyes and tapped her foot. Even in miniature that thing was a bitch.

"Fine. Okay, I get it. Assassin for hire. Go where the money takes you. Kill whatever or whoever you're told to kill." She turned to Alex and Ronan. "She's just a pawn. She doesn't know anything."

"Do, too," the pixie said, sounding smug.

"Uh-huh," Kali said in a voice that she hoped very clearly conveyed her disbelief. "Why would they tell you anything? You're obviously a very *small* part of a much bigger plot." She turned her back on the pixie, dismissing the creature's existence.

"Do you have any idea who I am?"

"Not a clue," Kali said over her shoulder. "Can't say I much care, either."

"I am Connistanterina Elizabeth DeKardoin, fourth-born daughter of the Pixie King. I am royalty, and you will treat me as such."

"Well, *Conni*," Kali said, hoping the shortening of her name would infuriate the woman enough for her to spill some useful information. "As royalty in the enemy camp, perhaps you should consider human history. I'm pretty sure we beheaded captured royals."

"Human barbarians. No sense of honor."

"Says the miniature assassin caught in a glass jar. You're pathetic. You talk of honor like you understand what it means."

"Of course I know what it means. The Oracle broke the rules. She intended to pass her information onto humans." The pixie spat the word "humans" like it was some despicable contagious disease. "I killed her to protect my people. If I had known the traitor was capable of passing her information to human babies, I would have killed them all that day."

"So you're not a hired assassin."

"I was not hired. I was chosen." The pixie stuck her nose in the air, her eyes shining with what could only be described as a fanatical light. It didn't matter what reasonable argument they made, this pixie had no intention of listening, ever. Considering she'd just announced she was willing to kill newborn babies, it took all of Kali's sense of humanity not to grab the jar and start shaking until the callous bitch cried.

"Why you?" Kali asked, trying to inject a mocking tone into her voice instead of the rage she felt. "What's so special about you? You don't look up to the job from where I'm standing."

"I am the best," the miniature pixie said with an arrogant sniff. "I grabbed the Oracle, transported her to a place with no paranormal creatures, and silenced her."

"But you failed, because she passed her knowledge on to humans." Kali tilted her head, lifting the jar to look more closely at the pixie. She could see the annoyance even on such a tiny face, but a theory was starting to solidify in her mind, and she decided to try and get confirmation. "You're cleaning up your own mess. Nobody even knows you're doing this. That's why the assassinations weren't simultaneous. You've been doing this on your own."

The pixie didn't say anything, but Kali could see the woman's fear now. It seemed pretty obvious that she had no backup. It was likely that no one would even notice that the pixie was missing—at least not for a while.

"Can pixies starve to death?"

"No," the pixie said with a half laugh that didn't quite hide her terror. "Unlike humans, we are not fragile creatures."

"Good to know," Kali said as she turned to her men. "How long will the wards stay in place?"

"Indefinitely," Alex said with a grim smile. Kali could sense the anger both her men were feeling toward the conscienceless assassin.

"Good," Kali said. She lifted the microphone away from the jar, glanced around the room, and finally settled on the cupboard under the kitchen sink. She found an old ceramic sugar container large enough to place the glass jar inside. The pixie was doing some sort of tantrum, but without the amplified sound Kali could barely hear a thing. "Maybe a few years of solitary confinement will help you to see the error of your ways. Good-bye, Conni."

She placed the lid on the pottery jar, placed the pottery under the sink, and closed the cupboard door. She turned to her men.

"Let's go home."

Chapter Eight

Kali glanced around her kitchen and wondered how everything that had happened in the past few days could suddenly feel like a dream. With Ronan and Alex in another room it almost felt like none of it had happened.

"You okay, sis?" Dave asked as he stepped into the small area.

"I think so," she said honestly.

"I want you to move in with Ronan." It was obvious that her brother had been beside himself with worry, and so she knew without a shadow of a doubt that he wanted her to move in with Ronan so that he could protect her. This wasn't another of Dave's lousy matchmaking moves. Although, considering that the last guy he'd set her up with was one of the two guys she was hopelessly in love with now, maybe his instincts hadn't been so lousy after all. "Even with the pixie locked away, there is no guarantee that you'll be safe. Alex says the wards will hold her, but he and Ronan don't want to alert anyone else to her whereabouts. The fewer people who know what happened to her or where she is the less likely she is to escape." He crossed his arms and gave her his worried-big-brother look. "But it's probably only a matter of time before someone else connects the dots and decides to finish what she started."

"I know all of that," she said quietly, trying not to convey her annoyance. Dave was just being her big brother and trying to protect her. He probably had no way of knowing how unbalanced she felt.

"Or would you rather move in with Alex?" Dave asked with a sympathetic smile. Hell, maybe he did know. She'd never really been able to hide anything from the brother who'd protected her all her life.

Smiling softly, she tried to find words to reassure him without quite confessing that she loved both Ronan and Alex. But again her big brother proved how well he knew her.

"Go talk to them." He pressed a kiss to her forehead. "And know that whatever way you choose to live your life you will always have my love and support." Tears blurred her vision, and she hugged her brother fiercely. After a few moments he laughed quietly. "If nothing else, it will make Thanksgiving rather interesting this year." She nodded, gave him a watery smile, and watched as he let himself out the front door.

"Dave heading home?" Ronan asked. She nodded. "Good, Alex and I want to run a few decisions by you."

"Decisions? Like what?"

"Like where we're going to live, beautiful," Alex said from the doorway of the living area. Her heart did a strange little tap dance before she could remind herself that they were only talking about protecting her long term. The three of them would probably have wild monkey sex to pass the time, but it was just fun. It wasn't the true relationship her heart wanted.

"We have a few choices," Ronan said, studying her face as if he could sense something was wrong but had no clue how to deal with it. "I have a number of safe houses dotted across several different countries."

"Or we could hide you in another realm," Alex added.

"Another realm? As in not on Earth?" It was probably stupid considering what she'd experienced in the past few days, but she'd never really considered the possibility of different planes of existence.

"Technically it is *on* Earth, but a place that exists in the same space yet in a different dimension."

"Huh?" Okay, maybe she should have read more paranormal or science fiction stories, but almost everything that Alex had just said seemed to be in a foreign language.

"Think of it as moving to another country with a different culture."

"Can't I just stay here?" Yes, as soon as the words came out of her mouth, she knew how stupid the request was. She was vulnerable here, that much was a given, but her life had changed so quickly there was a part of her that didn't want to let go. "I mean, what will I do? How will I survive? I can't live off you two for the rest of my life."

"Why not?" Ronan asked with genuine confusion. Hell, didn't he understand anything about her?

And then the most frightening thought of all finally sat up and smacked her in the face. No, he didn't know her. Neither did Alex. Hell, her life had been so far away from normal the past few days that she wasn't sure *she* even knew who she was. Fuck!

"I just can't. I need...my independence...my...my space." She stumbled over the words, regretting them the moment she glanced at Ronan's face. His expression didn't change, but he paled considerably. Alex looked ready to say something, but Ronan went into professional-soldier mode, and it suddenly felt like nothing they'd shared had been real.

"Okay, pack what you'll need. We move out in twenty minutes. I'll get the guys to set up a secure Internet link at the safe house in Texas. We'll make sure you're able to work while you're protected."

He left the room without looking at her once, his manner completely professional, but it was obvious that she'd hurt him deeply.

"I...I didn't..." She turned to Alex, unsure what expression she would find on his face. She'd likely hurt him with her poorly chosen words as well. What she found was the man with a wide grin, shaking his head in mock disappointment. Confused and maybe a little angry with his reaction, Kali crossed her arms and waited for him to say something.

"It's a complete mystery to me how you two even made it into the same car on your first date. I think it's quite a lucky thing you'll have me around to sort out the misunderstandings. Hell, once the children come along, it's liable to get worse."

"What?" Kali asked, shaking her head, utterly confused. "What children?"

"Yours and Ronan's of course. You know you're perfect for each other. He knows it, too, but somehow you two keep going all human and messing things up. At least with me around you'll be able to sort through the issues before they become insurmountable." She shook her head as the tears fell down her cheeks even as she cursed herself for letting her ragged emotions show. Alex pulled her into his embrace, hugging her tight as he became very serious. "Kali, you love him. You know you do."

"I know," she whispered, "but I love you, too."

"Good to know," he said with a quick squeeze. "So now all we have to do is convince the stubborn soldier that we can be a family."

"I need to go talk to him, don't I?"

"I've always found talking a very effective way of communicating," he said with a smile in his voice.

She sighed, hugged Alex closer, and whispered, "I didn't mean it the way it came out."

"I know, beautiful, but Ronan hates being vulnerable." She leaned back to see Alex's face. Ronan was a bossy, confident, well-trained soldier. Everything in his life was about maximizing his client's safety and minimizing vulnerability. But love wasn't a job. It wasn't even predictable. It was raw and messy and, in Kali and Ronan's case, filled with misunderstandings and hurt feelings.

Kali was still wondering how to deal with Ronan's reaction—and, yes, maybe even wondering how to protect herself from being vulnerable to him—when he came back into the room. His expression was quickly hidden, but the hurt in his eyes had been unmistakable.

"Ronan," Kali said, trying to shore up her courage and say what Ronan needed to hear. "I love you."

"It's okay, Kali," Ronan said, sounding like the soldier he was—professional, polite, and distant. "We'll make sure you're safe. You don't need to pretend."

The man was infuriating. "I'm not pretending." She wanted to stamp her foot like a five-year-old, but it probably wouldn't help convince him that she knew her own mind. The silly man had probably decided that what they'd shared at the cabin had simply been stress relief.

But as angry as she was feeling, that flash of hurt crossed his features again, and she wanted to grab him and shake him, and maybe kiss him all over, until he understood what she'd meant earlier.

"Ronan, I phrased it badly." She stood right in front of him and waited until he finally looked down at her. "I love you, and I love Alex, and while I might be stubborn enough to want to contribute to the family income, I want to do it as part of our family. *Our* family—yours, mine, and Alex's."

"You want to marry me?" His reaction seemed so shocked that Kali suddenly wondered if Alex had any clue what he was talking about. Maybe Ronan's reaction to her carelessly chosen words was him taking the opportunity to end things before they got too complicated. Pain, like a knife plunged through her chest, had her gasping for air. "Kali," Ronan said, sounding very serious once more. He lifted a hand to either side of her face, caressing her cheeks softly as a tear escaped her control and slid down her cheek. "Please marry me and Alex. Please have our babies. Please let us spend the rest of our lives sorting out the misunderstandings."

Alex moved to stand behind her, pressed a kiss to her shoulder, and repeated Ronan's words in a voice thick with emotion. "We both love you, Kali. Marry us, please."

Relief flooded through her as she fell more deeply in love with both her men. And then Kali nodded and said the only word zipping through her mind. "Yes."

Epilogue

"Okay," Alex said as he came through the front door. "Everything at the fortress is ready."

Kali smiled at the nickname he'd given the heavily protected home they were moving into. It was basically a house in the middle of a ghost town in the middle of nowhere, but it would be perfect for raising a family. Of course that was as long as they made her "death" believable. Between the three of them, they'd decided that she needed a new identity. Since nobody, other than the pixie who'd attacked her, knew what Kali looked like, they'd felt safe enough hiding her in plain sight but had decided that setting up a home in the tiny, deserted town of Sugarvale would offer added protection.

Alex's mission report had listed his protection detail as a complete failure. Kali had hated that he'd needed to blot his flawless work history, but as Alex had pointed out over and over, it was the report his supervisors had expected anyway. Nobody had ever managed to survive a pixie assassination once they'd been targeted. Only Kali's brother and Alex's PUP squad knew that she'd survived. Officially, even in human records, Kali had been one of the pixie's victims. The only person who could tell them otherwise was currently residing in a glass jar stored under a kitchen sink.

But it was very chilling to realize just how lucky she'd been— especially since they still hadn't been able to find the others. So far, Alex's PUP squad had only found one of the women on the list, and she'd already been targeted by the pixie. Hopefully Nathan and Brody would be able to explain the situation to Ava without scaring her to death. Then they somehow had to convince her to leave her old life behind just as Kali had done. Even if Kali was the Oracle's receptacle, Ava and the others would still be targets if anyone else noticed the pattern of the pixie's human murders and discovered the reason behind them.

"Ready to go?" Alex asked with a wicked smile.

"I guess so." Kali already felt green from the nausea the slip travel would cause. It had been a hectic twenty-four hours packing and getting ready to go and, other than a couple of unintentional catnaps, Kali hadn't slept. She was fairly certain that neither Alex nor Ronan had slept at all.

Alex leaned over and kissed her passionately, the breath-stealing kiss almost distracting her from the fact that Ronan had pressed up behind her, wrapped an arm around her middle, and pushed his hand down inside her jeans. The immediate arousal was surprising but definitely not unwelcome.

Ronan's thick fingers rubbed over her clit as Alex's tongue explored her mouth, and a hand squeezed her nipple so hard she'd swear she saw stars.

"Come for us," Ronan ordered. A moment later she wholeheartedly obeyed, the orgasm shockingly intense despite the rapid buildup, the rolling, shivering, rippling of ecstasy somehow magnified by the slip travel.

Shaking all over, Kali would have buckled at the knees if Alex and Ronan hadn't been holding her up.

"Bedtime," Ronan said, sounding quite tired. She felt pretty good, the nausea absent thanks to her orgasm, but it was obvious by the hard cock pressed against her ass that Ronan hadn't joined her in bliss.

"Good idea," Kali said. "A quick nap and then wild monkey sex."

"I'd prefer you had wild demon sex," Alex said with a wide grin. "But you primates can do whatever it takes."

They hadn't been able to track down any paranormal ancestors in Kali's line. Of course, the confirmation that she was fully human didn't quite explain the telekinesis or the "knowing" stuff that she probably shouldn't. Maybe she really was the Oracle's receptacle. Until they found the others, they had no idea if Kali was unique or not. Alex planned to speak to Brody and ask if Ava had any unusual skills, but with everything else going on it would be a few days more at least before her men were confident enough of their precautions to leave her with only one of them. They would figure out who or what she was eventually, but for now she wanted to concentrate on her men.

Alex smiled wickedly and pulled her from Ronan's arms. He caressed her breast as he whispered in a conspiratorial voice, "I want you two to practice baby making as often as possible so that when we decide to have a family, you'll know exactly what to do."

Kali laughed, glanced at Ronan, and noticed he didn't seem at all disturbed by the talk of babies this early in their relationship.

"Will do," she whispered back. "But there may be one little crimp in your plans."

Alex raised an eyebrow and waited for her to elaborate.

"Remember how I know stuff I probably shouldn't know but know anyway?" He nodded. "I know that humans and fire demons can't normally interbreed, but for some reason, you and I can."

"We can what?" Alex asked, looking adorable in his surprise.

"We can have babies together, Alex. I don't really understand how it's possible. I just know it is."

"We can be a real family?" Alex asked excitedly.

Ronan grinned, slapped his friend on the back, and kissed Kali softly. "I'll meet you in bed."

Kali nodded, grateful for Ronan's understanding. Alex had seemed so self-assured, so confident in his place in their relationship, that Kali hadn't really given any thought to the emotions he'd kept hidden. Judging by his reaction to her announcement, he'd seen himself as some sort of second-string husband and not an equal partner.

"Alex," she said as he sat on the sofa and pulled her onto his lap.

"Yes, beautiful?"

"You know that I'll always love you and Ronan equally, don't you?"

"You know, I would have answered yes to that question a few hours ago, but it would seem that a part of me truly didn't believe it."

"But you believe it now?"

"Absolutely. Kali, I've felt a connection to you since the moment we met. It doesn't matter if they're human babies or demon babies. I promise to love them all and love their mother always."

"I love you, Alex."

"I love you, too, beautiful. Let's go get some sleep."

Kali glanced over to see Ronan's smile widen before he winked and stepped from the room.

Several hours later, wedged tightly between the men who loved her, Kali fell asleep with a smile on her lips and joy in her heart. This was where she belonged. It didn't matter where they lived. It only mattered that they were together.

THE END

WWW.ABBYBLAKE.BLOGSPOT.COM

ABOUT THE AUTHOR

Abby Blake prefers to read or write romance over just about everything else—except maybe chocolate. Most days she can be found hurrying to do what needs to be done so that she can curl up with her laptop and her latest bunch of heroes.

Also by Abby Blake

Ménage Everlasting: PUP Squad Alpha 3: *Dragon's Fire*
Ménage Everlasting: PUP Squad Alpha 4: *Bears' Claim*
Ménage Everlasting: PUP Squad Alpha 5: *Warlock's Way*
Ménage Everlasting: PUP Squad Alpha 6: *Wolves' Bite*
Ménage Everlasting: PUP Squad Alpha 7: *Angel's Touch*
Ménage Everlasting: PUP Squad Alpha 8: *Oracles' Light*

For all other titles, please visit
www.bookstrand.com/abby-blake

Siren Publishing, Inc.
www.SirenPublishing.com

CPSIA information can be obtained at www.ICGtesting.com
Printed in the USA
LVOW12s1840220614

391148LV00029B/1286/P

9 781622 413362